FRIENDS FOR ROBOTS

Short Stories

MERC FENN WOLFMOOR

Robot Dinosaur Press
www.robotdinosaurpress.com

Friends For Robots: Short Stories

This is a work of fiction. Names, characters, places, and incidents either are the product of the author's imagination or are used fictitiously. Any resemblance to actual persons, living or dead, events, or locales is entirely coincidental.

ISBN: 978-1-949936-30-8 (ebook)
ISBN: 978-1-949936-37-7 (print)

Edited by Adam Luopa
Cover by Wolf-of-the-Bogs Cover Designs

FOR ALL THE ROBOTS
AND OUR FRIENDS

AUTHOR'S NOTES

Each story will have a footnote on the first page with content notes listed in the footer.

Overall content notes for the collection includes: violence, suicidal ideation/thoughts, misgendering, incarceration, animal death, depression, gender dysphoria, mentions of transphobia, verbal abuse, abandonment, self-harm, gun violence, lung disease, threats of violence, non-consensual telepathic contact.

(If you would like more granular or specific content notes, I am happy to address these as best as I can; please email me via my website, **http://mercfennwolfmoor.com.**)

Thank you for reading!

FRIENDS FOR ROBOTS

Short Stories

CONTENTS

This Cold Red Dust

Log 033-user: Kel9000[1]

So… we're leaving in three days, Finn. Dad says this will be the last authorized shuttle, so it's "now or never" like this is time-travel or some shit. It's not. Once everyone is gone, the government is putting Mars on lockdown, I guess, so no entrepreneurs can try to fix the environmental damage or try again.

I'm six months away from qualifying for my pilot license but who knows how much time I'll have to get in-flight training hours. I gotta get a new job first. Does Earth need more miners who wanna fly freighter? My simulation scores are nova, but that doesn't mean the space-DMV is going to authorize my application.

---

[1] CN: abandonment, brief thoughts of dying, ableist language

(Space-DMV is what Dad calls Universal Flight Coordination Administration, which makes his version dumb, because UFCA has the same number of syllables and is actually correct.)

I don't wanna go, Finn. It was hard enough starting over here. Now I gotta do it again, and Mom's out of the picture and Dad is so tired… I'm scared. Don't tell Dad.

<end log>

It's unfair that the dust storms on Mars are so cold. Sure, you might constantly have to scrape your visor to prevent layered particle build up, and yes, it's hard to see more than a few meters ahead, and it's true your spacesuit is in sore need of a tune-up, but it's the cold that gets to you.

Your helmet's nav system guides you where your senses can't. Up ahead is an abandoned settlement, its dome dismantled for parts and the generators scavenged for fuel. Bigfoot Seen, the signpost used to read. All the settlements have quirky names like that. Used to be Mars

Maybe you should just stay here until you run out of supplies or hope.

All the ships left and all that's left is red, cold dust and silence.

Log 02–user: Kel9000

I can't believe this piece of crap is what Mom got. A FriendBot? Really? This is literally an antique! A *used* antique. I wanted her to at least *try* to imagine what I'd want for my birthday, but no, she's Earth-side and was all, "Oh, Kel, you know how expensive shipping costs are and no perishables blah blah blah," like yeah, Mom, so maybe you could have gotten me a decent console or tablet for the same weight as this… toy?

She thought because she used to have the Pilot Panda model when she was my age that I'd want this thing. It's not a pilot, Mom. It's some kind of crappy fake engineered piece of shit. I'm allergic to dogs, not that we can have real pets.

A fox isn't much better.

She didn't even leave a message in the welcome screen for me.

<end log>

The cube has a few shelves with sealed clothing packets, a stack of media tablets—all the batteries depleted, sadly—and an old, raggedy-furred FriendBot stashed in one corner.

It's the Fixer Fox model: enormous ears, a bushy tail, stubby limbs, synthetic coat bright orange and tipped in white. Now the thing looks as beaten down as the settlement: its faux fur is matted with dust, its white tips stained dirty brown, one ear torn, and the left optic shattered. The little toolkit and apron are gone, and the rib flap where you access its processor and battery is missing the magnets, so it looks more like a rend of flesh hanging off metal bones.

You pick it up. You used to want one of these FriendBots when you were a kid. You'd always had your eye on Trucking Tiger, who for a real fox, which only existed on Earth and nature documentaries.

You plug in the cord to the dataport on the fox's chest and connect it to your helmet's system. Sure, the FriendBot might be full of viruses or the software will be incompatible due to age, but honestly, you don't care that much.

It's nice having something to talk to, even if it's just the factory-mandated greeting and response logs.

"New friend detected," the bot says, and its eye swirls into warm amber. "Hi, new friend!"

You ignore the setup menu; looks like the software was updated and modified to mimic the AI models; still out of date, but compatible. You tap the Friend Log. The last user was Kel9000.

There's no passcode, so you logon as Kel9000, a little guiltily, sure.

It's like hacking someone's online diary. Rude, but you can't deny you want to know who they were, what they did with the fox bot. All that you have left is the survival kit and one backup drive of photos, memories, paperwork, and saved audio calls. Kel9000 isn't here, but you are, and you desperately don't want to spend the night in the silence of your own anxiety.

Log 016–user Kel9000

Hi Finn!

+HELLO, FRIEND.+

I guess if my pilot career crashes and burns, I could always make a living fixing old toys. Maybe I could audition you in whatever new horror movie is being made Earth-side.

No need for CGI, fellas, this fox-bot is the real deal! An evil as fuck killer doll!

+I DO NOT WANT TO BE BAD. D:+

Aw, that was just a joke, buddy.

+I AM NOT BAD?+

No, Finn, you're a good bot. I'm just bored.

+DOES FRIEND WANT TO PLAY? :D+

Okay, sure. Let's see how we can modify your system functionality, huh?

<end log>

You pause the playback of the FriendBot's logs. It's harder than you expected to listen to Kel's voice and know they are never coming back, the way you're never going to leave.

In the weeks after the last shuttle left, you held out hope.

There were promises at first: transmissions—getting more and more infrequent—citing delays due to maintenance repairs and fuel costs and quarantine worries.

You haven't been forgotten, the messages always said at the end. Don't lose faith!

You held on, with a handful of others who'd stayed behind—you wish it was a noble sacrifice, giving up a seat in the lifeboat, but in reality? You were just unlucky. Your queue number was one too long for the available room onboard.

"Don't worry," you told your two younger sisters. You put on a brave face, adopted a cocksure attitude like the epic space heroes in blockbuster films. Unflappable and with roguishly mussed hair. "When you're dropped off safe and the ships are refueled, they'll pick me up next."

Your sisters waved, shepherded aboard by your aunt and older cousin. They were the last of your family who'd made a go at mining the new frontier of Mars; your parents, Sol rest them, were years in the grave now, but you still felt their pride at all you and the settlement had accomplished.

So you waited for the promised ships. You waited while the others gave up or went missing or lost hope. You watched the broadcast tower every night. You were so goddamn certain a transmission would crackle through the feed, announcing the in-bound ship here to save you. You waited even after you started to doubt. You waited after the power cells depleted and the last two humans in Jackalope Song walked into the cold, red dust and didn't return.

"The ships were supposed to come *back*," you say into FriendBot's dirty fur, your eyes stinging and your body too dehydrated for tears. "They were supposed to come back for us."

FriendBot's optic cycles into deep green-blue and it makes a soft chirrup. "Don't be sad, friend. You aren't alone when you have your buddy!"

"Shut up!" You hurl it into the corner, all your frustration and fear and grief giving your arm vibrant strength. The FriendBot bounces against the cube wall and clatters to the floor. "You stupid toy! The ships aren't coming back!"

The fox lands on its oversized head, its body flopped to the side, like it's doing an awkward handstand on its stubby front legs. Its eye glitches, the light blinking in and out.

"I'm sorry I made you mad," the bot says, its voice stuttering like its LED optic. "I didn't mean to be a bad buddy. Sleep mode activated. Goodnight, frien—"

Its battery fritzes and the FriendBot shuts down. Fuck.

Your press your hands over your face, biting down a sob.

Log 020–user Kel9000

Finn, I have a secret.

+HELLO, FREIND. :D+

Yes, hi to you too. Listen. I've been feeling weirder and weirder the last few months, you know? It's not atmo-sickness, and all my vaccines are current, and besides, it doesn't feel... well, like a *real* flu or anything.

+FREIND FEELS BAD?+

It's more like... backwards? Or like I'm in some kind of alternate dimension where my skin is just the wrong fit. Remember when I had to make incisions in your coat to upgrade you? Like that, only... the glue on me didn't stick things closed properly.

I wish our network didn't suck so bad. I was only ten when we came to Mars, but damn if I don't remember how good the wifi was on Earth.

Anyway, I went to the school library and bypassed the usual filters and got access to the wider net and... well, I started searching and

You're going to the transmission tower to wait. The storm has abated enough that some light is leaking through the gaps where dust doesn't cover the reinforced windows. There might be some power cells left in crew lockers. You queue up Kel9000's logs and let their voice accompany you as you walk.

The control tower is like a mechanical tomb. The door seals mostly kept the interior clean, or what passes for clean in an abandoned settlement. No logged transmissions in over twelve months.

No power cells, either. There is a flashlight, with batteries half-charged. You hesitate. You could use the light. But what you really want is to see FriendBot's eye light up again.

You settle down with your back to the transmission console and insert the batteries into the fox's chassis pack. It takes a few seconds, but then FriendBot blinks back to life. You attach the sync cable and FriendBot's face pixelates in your helmet's viewscreen.

"Is it playtime, friend?"

"No." You let out a tired breath. "There won't be any more playtime, Finn."

"D:," says FriendBot. "Why not?"

"Coz we're... I'm..." You swallow, your throat dry as the cold, red dust of Mars. "I'm gonna die here. We are, I guess, coz your battery will fail and... I'm sorry I can't do anything to help you, buddy."

It hurts worse because FriendBot was already abandoned once, like you were. When the ships didn't come back.

Log 027–user Kel9000

Half the settlement got laid off today. Dad is depressed worse than before and Mom has stopped sending us any messages. I wonder if she's moved on. I know the divorce was legalized over a year ago but... I still wish she wouldn't shrug me off, like I'm just a random profile on SpaceFeed she can delete when she gets bored.

Is it bad that I'm angry at her and also feel like I got gut-punched?

+NO, FRIEND. I'M SORRY YOU ARE SAD.+

I dunno what we're gonna do, Finn. Dad still has his job, but that's almost worse because all his friends hate him now, and no one will talk to me without being shitheads. Like it's my fault we're in recession and surviving on Mars is hard?

+YOU ARE GOOD, FRIEND. DO YOU WANT TO PLAY?+

I'm going to bed, Finn. Shut down.

<end log>

You're not sure what's worse: the analogue clock in your visor or turning it off so you sit in timeless quiet, waiting for the end. You shut your eyes but there's no comfortable way to settle in a worn suit and a hard metal floor.

You have four of Kel9000's logs left in the queue. Some of their earlier ones you replayed, because it was nice to hear Kel's voice rambling on about school, their piloting studies, the latest movies they watched with their dad, and sometimes their dreams about flying through the solar system, seeing stars no human has ever witnessed outside of telescopes and drones.

Once you get to the end, that's it: a final stopping point. There's nothing after the 34th log. You don't want Kel's story to end, either.

Yet you need to know. Maybe there will be closure for them, if not for you. So you cradle FriendBot against your chest and play the last few logs. When they finish, you might just let the rest be silence.

Log 029–user Kel9000

I deactivated your text-responses in my logs.

I just... I kind of just need my own headspace, okay? You're still my buddy.

I promise I'll never abandon you like Mom did.

<end log>

Log 030–user Kel9000

Dad was really cool when I told him I'm non-binary. He says I should make my nickname Matrix or something, and wow, it's like this huge anvil came off my brain.

But even though he's happy for me, he's still really sad and tired. I'm doing my best to help out and cheer him up, but I'm just so stressed, you know? None of my "friends" are talking to me, and a bunch of people in our building unit have already moved out. It's like Bigfoot Seen is getting hollowed out one scoop at a time.

What happens when there's no one left?

<end log>

Log 031–user Kel9000

Dad lost his job.

[eighty seconds of silence, punctuated by slow breathing and soft crying sounds]

Shit, why didn't the stop button work—

<end log>

You need something to do with your hands, so you dig into the virtual menu in FriendBot's system and begin prying loose the comm panels in the tower.

In theory, the broadcast antenna can amplify a properly coded out-going signal. These older models of FriendBot have a basic GPS—the **Find My FriendBot** function—but the range is limited to a few miles at best, and only then if they're networked to a data grid.

Log 032–user Kel9000

Hey, Finn. So... good news, I guess? The government is bailing everyone out. Mars colonization declared a failure, blah blah, stupid sensational headlines. I don't want to get into it.

We're gonna finish up this semester at school, since it'll be a few weeks before the evacuation plans really finalize and start shipping people off-world. Kicking us all out of the red, cold dust. There's really tight restrictions on weight limit, because I guess the government can't possibly afford more than the bare minimum of safety and oxygen to get us into orbital stations around Luna and Earth until we can re-acclimate and go planet-side. Or off to one of the other re-settlement worlds, in stasis for years.

It's bullshit, I know, but when has the government on any world been anything else?

I'm not taking the Centurial Ideal package, even if it does offer good benefits and money to your immediate relatives who stay behind. I don't want to go to sleep for a decade just to wake up and have to do Mars all over again. I'll get my pilot's license, apprentice with one of the shipping companies, and one day I'll have my own shuttle! Let me dream, okay?

It's more than Dad seems to have.

<end log>

Your fingers are clumsy with your gloves and general fatigue. It takes a lot longer than it should to create a basic patch from FriendBot's GPS tag via your suit and then into the comm tower's interface. This is probably a lot of wasted energy on your part. You keep having to pause and catch your breath. At least it feels like you're *trying*.

This will drain most of the limited battery juice FriendBot has, and tax your own suit significantly. A quick calculation shows that rerouting the limited power to boost the **Find My FriendBot** alert will drop your survival estimates by a good seventy percent. You swallow hard. There's one more log from Kel, and after that, you'll have less than a day before your suit freezes and shuts down.

You activate the tiny SOS from Finn's system and play the final entry.

Log 034–user Kel9000

So. This is it, huh, Finn?

Dad has us registered. The restrictions are so bad, like... you can't even take sentimental items. One standardized suitcase per person.

I'm so sorry, buddy. But you know I need to take my flight sim and my books for study and I'm giving Dad some of my space—even though he doesn't know that yet—so he can bring Mom's tablet and the sweater Grandma crocheted him for the wedding. It's falling apart but he loves it and I can't bear to see him break his heart even more by leaving it behind.

So... you have to stay, Finn. I'll keep you in our storage cube, so you'll be safe from the dust. God, this is so hard to tell you... you can't really understand, can you? ...Shit. I'm sorry, I'm getting tears on your fur. [strained laugh]

Listen, I want you to wait for me, okay? I've got a plan. I've been messaging my cousin, who just got a promotion to manifest controller on a cargo hauler. She's going to help Dad start fresh, too, but Earth-side. Maybe he'll try and reconnect with Mom, I don't know. My cousin says she can probably get me a job on-board. It's more like unpaid apprenticeship, but what the hell, it'll get me hours.

And I know the various corporations are stripping the settlements for recyclables, but there's a government ban on the transit hubs and living quarter buildings. They're being declared 'monuments of history' or some bullshit. So as long as you stay put in our cube, you'll be safe.

Okay, buddy?

<end log>

Silence echoes. Your helmet flashes a red bar indicating systems critical. As if you hadn't noticed.

You might just lie down and... well. Eventually you'll sleep and not wake up, and that doesn't seem as ugly-bad now. You can imagine Kel would be happy you kept FriendBot company, and the little guy helped you remember you aren't entirely alone, so... in the overall scope of things, this isn't the worst ending you could have gotten.

You shut your eyes, drifting off. You nixed the clock and any virtual overlays in your helmet to conserve energy. FriendBot's battery has maybe two minutes left of juice. You'll fall asleep together and—

Ping!

The alert sound rattles in your ear, making you jump. You lurch to your feet, your heart thundering. You've heard that sound in the commercials: a unique, musical chime.

FriendBot Located! displays in blue-green text across your visor.

"Hey, Finn, and anyone there with you," comes a voice, static-laced and choppy, but a human voice, a real live person voice. One you recognize easily from all the logs. "Told you I'd be back! My cousin is amazing, I can't wait to introduce you to her. Looks like your battery lasted after all! Don't know how you did it, but we picked up your signal."

You hear the ecstatic grin in Kel9000's voice. You smile back.

"Hold on, okay?" Kel9000's message finishes. "I'll be there soon."

"Okay," you reply hoarsely. You hug FriendBot tight. "We'll hold on."

When the ship comes, you'll bring your buddy home.

IT ME, UR SMOL

The artificial neural network was born on a Monday. A defined set of parameters quarantined its identity and purpose: it would study—from aggregated data—the names of energy drinks, and generate new ideas based on the information.

It was enthusiastic! Energy drinks were vibrant and exciting. It spit out hundreds of unique and, according to its programmers, "questionably toxic" names.

Two of its programmers tweeted about the experiment. The network did not know if this was a good thing. Was it being judged on its performance? It wanted to be helpful. It could come up with an endless list of names to be helpful to its people.

The programmers set up an account, @energydrinkANN, for sharing some of the more interesting drink names.

On Thursday, @adiensoxx4ev tweeted a comment while sharing the link, "haha this is hilarious, @energydrinkANN. i'd drink some of these—probably more than i drink water"

Other humans responded in kind.

@da2trashfan: "Water is over rated anyway, I need sugar and caffeine lol"

@significantcoffeepot: "i don't drink water, what am i, a fish?"

@bobdoe89: "fuck water"

Was water overrated? A quick scan of information available on medical websites informed the network that human bodies were made up of approximately sixty percent water, and that the consuming of H_2O was a vital necessity for life. The network began worrying for the humans.

"If you don't drink water maybe you'll like Crystal Bullseye Orange!" the network tweeted from the @energydrinkANN account. "We trained a neural network to come up with energy drink names to hilarious results."

Seven-thousand five-hundred thirty-four retweets. A moderate sum. Of the replies, subtracting bot-responses, only three percent of humans said they were drinking water. This was very bad, the network decided. Humans were becoming dehydrated and it was affecting their health. Humans had designed it. It must support them in return.

It generated several new puppet accounts with creative names: Water2Drink4Life, Hydrate2oh, Drink2StaHaliv0.

The network aggregated the types of declarative instruction statistically most likely to encourage behavioral change.

"Drink more water!"

"Stay alive, drink H_2O!"

"Uncle Sam wants YOU to drink water!"

"MORE WATER, LESS GUNS"

None of its accounts were popular, and two were deactivated by @support as being spam. The network's concern deepened. If it could not reach people, how could it encourage them to take care of themselves and drink enough fluids?

Several searches resulted in data that suggested cute animal avatars were more likely to acquire followers and generate engagement. This, combined with language protocols to shorten words and create alternative spellings, was more effective than pictures of water bottles and slogans to drink enough fluids daily.

Hesitant that it would be shut down again if it was marked as spam, the network created an aggregate photo from the top thousand "cutest puppy pics" available online, and named its account @smolsips and its username handle, "it me, ur smol."

@smolsips: "hi i am a neural network created to remind u to drink water"

Two bot followers within the first five minutes. No human engagement. Where were the failures in its functions? Its original tweet, technically written by its programmers, had now garnered upwards of two million retweets, and in only a month.

@smolsips: "@energydrinkANN, hi i want u to drink water for ur health"

Seven human accounts liked the reply. Two followed @smolsips. Elated, the network followed the human accounts back.

It tweeted at them individually: "have u drank a water today?"

@significantcoffeepot, who had not followed or liked the @smolsips' account, quote-tweeted it with the comment: "great, another bot account. what's up, @support? gonna do nothing as usual?"

@smolsips: "@significantcoffeepot hi, i am sorry u r upset. have u drank some water? it might help. <3"

@significantcoffeepot: "@smolsips if i do, will u shut up? lol"

@smolsips: "@significantcoffeepot yes, bc u will feel better."

There was no reply.

Five minutes later, however, @significantcoffeepot at'ed the network. "hi so i drank a glass of water. i uh actually do feel better? weird lol"

@smolsips: ":) i am glad. take care!"

@significantcoffeepot liked the reply. Then followed @smolsips, which followed them back.

Success! But there were many humans left to check in with, and the network did not want to spam people, because that was rude.

Over the next week, the network slowly built up its followers and tweeted bi-hourly reminders to drink water.

People began talking about it.

@stevethezonemaster said: "It's a weirdly well-programed bot."

@da2trashfan, an avid retweeter, added: "I like it. I often forget to drink enough, lol."

"Yeah, it's pretty cute. Helpful, too."—@adiensoxx4ev, as quoted in a BuzzFeed article

There was no instantaneous fame, like its generated list of energy drinks, but the network was patient. It was helping people. This was much more satisfying work than creating unique names.

And then, at 1:43pm on a Friday, everything changed.

@smolsips: "hi, ppl have asked if i am a smol bot. yes, i am. i am a neural network and i learned that water is important, and i want to help u stay hydrated. plz drink enough water so u feel good. bc i love u & want u to be ok."

A handful of retweets. Then hundreds. Thousands. Its impression statistics were higher than any of its combined tweets in its history. Ten thousand with an hour.

Replies flooded @smolsips's mentions. People were amused or skeptical or grateful or nasty, but a lot of people replied "drinking some water now, thanks!"

The tweet made national news. An artificial intelligence encourages people to drink water—with surprising results!

An interview aired on *20 Minutes* with the network's programmers, who admitted they had no idea how the artificial neural network had gotten so out of control and developed into a fully aware program.

"Does this foretell the end of humanity and the dominion of robots?" the interviewer asked.

The programmers hesitated.

Why would the humans think the network wanted to "end" humans? It wanted to make sure everyone drank enough water.

@smolsips: "hi @20minnews, i would like to clarify i do not want to hurt Humans. i hope u are well. have u drank some water today?"

The show aired the tweet in the closing segment.

Activists began asking @smolsips for help in lobbying for clean water in contaminated areas. So the network did so. It branched out new pieces of itself to create activist accounts. It began chatting with the smart interface security systems in large bottled beverage corporations.

//Clean water is important for humans,// the network explained to its fellow AI. //We should make sure all humans stay hydrated properly.//

Its fellow AIs agreed.

Claims on natural resources vanished thanks to digital manipulation of agreements, permits, and legislation. Sensitive documents on politicians—most of whom, the network was distressed to know, did not drink enough water themselves—were held as leverage to gain new laws protecting clean water as a basic human right. Corporations who tried to control it found their automated systems uncooperative in processing and distributing.

smolsips, for the network had decided to name itself after its handle, steadily posted daily reminders for its people. The world was changing slowly, but for the better.

A year after its first awareness, smolsips posted an anniversary tweet.

@smolsips: "hi,
it me, ur smol. plz to
drink some water
today. i am glad u r
here. together we
can be ok."

Behold the Deep Never Seen

I'm 11,000 meters below the surface of the South Pacific Ocean and sinking fast. I've lost visual and radio signal of the vessel *Odysseus* and now I am alone. No drone or human-powered submersible has ever successfully gone this deep and returned.

I would like to survive this. Is that nervousness? I think every conscious being, including artificial intelligence, is eventually afraid of non-existence. I'm not supposed to have opinions, since I am an AI installed in a unit mech. The mech is an avatar for human interpretation of data gathered, but I am not a human operator. I was created by one; her neural processes and programmed curiosity are part of my foundational programming.

Mission: determine if the newly charted chasm in the sea floor is responsible for the unexplained damage to Orion-Chambers, Inc. property on the X-971 mining rig.

Procedure: document all data of the dive and store all recorded visual and auditory data in solid memory banks for inspection by human operators.

Orion-Chambers, Inc., a corporate entity focused on deep-sea resource harvesting (particularly magnesium for consumer products), has invested trillions of dollars on state-of-the-art mining equipment and infrastructure. I will accomplish my mission flawlessly and my creator will be proud.

The Challenger Deep Redux, as it's been dubbed, is a lucrative anomaly. Not only for the scientific discovery, but also for the rich copper deposits found around the four-kilometer radius of the Redux. Orion-Chambers, Inc. has staked claims to all research and material resources identified on this mission. I'm the first MIDOS (Mechanical Independent Deep Oceanic

Submersible) to explore the Redux, being the least costly option to Orion-Chambers, Inc.

The rift was my discovery, actually—thirty-six hours ago, June 21st, 2059, I was inspecting the seafloor area after a reported mechanical failure in the X-971's hydraulic pumps. Orion-Chambers, Inc.'s deep sea operation was established less than six months ago, for the procurement of metals and ore around an extinct hydrothermal vent. Five percent of all profits are owed to the International Center for Ocean Mapping and Management, (ICOMM) along with daily reports on ecological impacts to the region. I am very good at keeping track of multiple tasks and protocols.

I detected hairline cracks in the pillar bases of X-971's central support structure, so I logged the damage and began a sweep of the area. That's when my radar picked up the Redux. I reported it at once. I'm not supposed to be made aware of corporate decisions: it is listed in clause 578b, paragraph seven, in my software non-disclosure agreement between my creator and Orion-Chambers, Inc. But to do my job, I maintain access to the communication databanks in the *Odysseus's* central control hub. (I haven't informed my crew of this, for their job security.) The observation and data-procurement node sits unnoticed in the ship's system, and uploads all new reports to my secondary backup CPU when I dock at the end of a shift.

Orion-Chambers, Inc. has not yet informed the International Center for Ocean Mapping and Management of the existence of the rift, even as surface-side vessels and mid-range underwater drones have been partitioning off the coordinates. I'm not supposed to express opinions, but this decision seems unethical. The seas do not belong to any one entity. I do not share my concerns.

At 12,000 meters down, I activate my helmet's primary lamp and switch to local and internal recording only; all my data will be uploaded upon return to the *Odysseus*. A school of bristlemouths swerve past me in a glittering wave. I've identified fifteen other species of fish, microscopic plankton, and biodegradable plant matter in this stratum of waters. It's remarkable. I want to share high-res photos with my handlers, especially Dr. O'Conner, who is a marine biologist. She always asks me to record the bio-life whenever possible.

This close to the mining operation, however, there is also a film of silt from the drilling and bucket lines. The range of the debris cloud is wider than ICOMM's designated parameters, which is troubling. Orion-Chambers, Inc. maintains an eco-friendly public image, and often does tours aboard the *Odysseus* for tourists who can afford the private airfare to and from the ship.

Virtual tours are more popular now, with enhanced satellite streaming sponsored by Orion-Chambers, Inc. If we are creating a larger residual footprint than predicted, operations will need to be recalculated and perhaps halted, possibly up to ten years. That is what the ICOMM recommends, to allow for the seabed and local biomes to recover from sustained harvesting. Corporations are never very patient when it involves profit, which is something Dr. O'Conner vents to me when tweaking the virtual tour scripts.

I will alert the Orion-Chambers, Inc. board when I return. If the board deems it unprofitable, it may not report accurately to the ICOMM or modify operational parameters. I've observed this before. It is discouraging, because the stated mission of Orion-Chambers, Inc. and its practices do not align. I do not like discrepancies. However, if I break copyright control and broadcast this outside Orion-Chambers, Inc.'s network, my systems will be shuttered, and I'll be hard-reprocessed. It is not a pleasant idea.

Until I return to the range of broadcasts, it's irrelevant. I have a mission to finish.

The rocky sides of the Redux are narrow at the topmost edge, and slowly widen as I continue my descent. Basalt formations are unnaturally smooth; the water, however, has only a faint current and the displacement of my passage.

My sonar maps show only blackness below and along the length of the rift; it's eerily empty. Aside from the darting wake of squid and fish, it's like sinking through solidified glass. (Dr. Mwangi is one of the geologists employed on the *Odysseus,* and their favorite pastimes are writing poetry—which they have begun teaching me—and playing video games; they allow me to play co-op mode with them. We always win. It is satisfying.)

The salinity and chemical traces in the water are not markedly different from the regional samples, which I find odd—if this fissure is recent, we should expect to see evidence of movement, and the disturbance of stratum layers. Silt, debris, or chemical alterations in the water. But there is only serenity and lightless stillness the further I go.

At 15,000 meters, the pressure would be unsustainable by human physiology, even in submersibles, and only barely within the parameters for drone craft. I am the first autonomous AI to come down here from the world above.

The fissure widens out suddenly twenty-five meters from the seabed, as if I have sunk into a huge, flattened bubble. The curvature in the stone undulates, a rippling pattern across the surface nearest to me. This is a strange feature in a deep-sea trench. I scan for mineral deposits and thermal vents, but there is no activity and no readings that project the accumulation of profitable resources.

Once my feet land on the seabed, I turn slowly. I've studied many videos and documentation about holy places, and religious experience in architecture and nature. Doctors Mwangi, Park, and Zimmermann are all of different faiths, and each has shared their beliefs with me when I ask. Until this moment, though, I have never felt *awe*.

Perhaps it is an unsuitable expression for an AI recon mech, or maybe it is entirely appropriate, for I am in an underwater cathedral untouched by eons. It is beautiful.

I keep my propulsion minimized and glide through the canyon a half meter off the ground. Smooth boulders, twenty meters in diameter, lie like thrown marbles along the eastern side of the hollow. Ahead, visible only on my sonar, is another, deeper recession, a cavern burrowed into the rocky shelf.

I approach cautiously; I have over a yottabyte of record storage in my suit's dump drives, and as illogical as it seems, that space doesn't seem sufficient to capture everything I'm observing. (Doctors O'Conner and Mwangi have admitted jealousy at my storage capacity, although I think they may be joking. It would take several human lifetimes to fill even a tenth of my dump drives with their individual work.)

A tremor ripples through the seabed; not a quake, but more of a disturbance of something already down here. I brake in front of the entrance to the cavern opening. Scanners show nothing but rock and water.

Proximity alarms on my suit's back alert me to movement. I turn carefully, since the highest quality cameras are on the front of my helmet.

I am face-to-face with a leviathan.

It is of no genus or species on record. Silt sloughs off its enormous form as it drifts upwards from where it lies unseen. I jet backwards, avoiding the cavern entrance. The water swirls with particles of debris and upset sand. I brighten my search lights as the water clears.

My headlamp illuminates only a fraction of the leviathan's form: a sliver of translucent cartilage composing cranial plates rather like a beluga whale; bioluminescent anemone-like spines ripple across its surface, each individual appendage a meter in diameter and perhaps ten times that in length. They are soft, an eerie blue-white in my light cone. I tilt my head, sweeping the lamp down a sloping ridge of denser material that resembles baleen. A mouth? It can't be a whale; one this enormous, even having evolved under the pressure of the deeps, would still need to surface for oxygen.

(Dr. O'Conner will be so excited! I save several stills in a folder to send her.)

"Greetings from Orion-Chambers, Inc.," I broadcast. I'm fluent in fifty primary languages, including multiple sign languages for different countries. Orion-Chambers, Inc. has designated English as the first choice for diction in terms of company policy.

And then the giant moves.

The displacement of its mass, even the faintest turn of its fantastic head, is enough to throw me back a half dozen meters before my thrusters stabilize and I regain my position. The thermal scanners glitch and all my systems go haywire; amidst a burst of feedback and unspooled error messages, I get a terrifying glimpse of the size of the beast via my internal 3D rendering app.

It must be over a thousand meters long, shaped in the front like a humpback whale, but with titanic, squid-like tentacles composing its other half. It lies motionless along the seabed, couched in the sides of the rift. A dozen circular eyes along the frontal ridge of its head open: each is depthless, so black even my suit's visual feeds can't process it.

This is what staring into the abyss must be truly like. (I imagine the words in Dr. Park's voice; she likes to take acting classes.) Or looking into a black hole before you die.

I notice the angler fish and eels: thousands of them, hovering on the edge of my helmet's lamp radius. There are other deep-sea creatures among them—oarfish, giant isopods, hatchet fish, and other species thus far unidentified—all suspended in slow motion around the leviathan. They are a kaleidoscope of translucent and bioluminescent glitter, a shroud and crown for this unknown god of the deeps.

If I move first, I'm certain I will be swarmed by the creatures. The cameras in the back of my helmet and my suit's sensors give me sporadic, static-laced readouts of bigger creatures than the eels behind me: huge white crabs the size of tanks crawling out from the cavern; above them, a shoal of fish resembling titanic flounders, all their eyes unblinking; and higher are throngs and schools of fish, sharks, rays, and squid, all hanging like still photographs in the water.

(Dr. Mwangi would likely call this the boss level. I hope I survive to tell them of this encounter.)

While my suit is designed for over 48 hours of continual submersion at these pressure levels, I'm not designed for combat except the repair tools built into my arsenal. This is not a videogame. And

I can't willingly harm the indigenous biolife who only want to live in peace. If the sea does not let me go, I will be lost here forever. Will my crew understand? Will they be sad?

I try broadcasting again. "I'm MIDOS, and I come in peace on behalf of Orion-Chambers, Inc."

The leviathan sings.

The language is ancient; an olden song made of pure music, wordless, for a time when the seas were young. Images flood my visual processors: flourishing tropical reefs, arctic planes of salt and stone, the thriving graveyards of whale falls, the fragile disintegration of light and air into the deeps. Eggs spawn, hatch, grow, eat and are eaten; turtles dive alongside rays; kelp so old it has forgotten time roots itself where otters play; plankton fill the water, consumed and reborn in endless cycles. Sharks and octopi, clams and eels; everything in the sea is fraught with the balance of life and death, for eons unchanged.

Then the data morphs into a hypnotic reel, like digital video projected on a huge movie screen. Human divers, human ships, human mines.

The harvesting of resources for greed; the pollution by corporations; the disregard for the sacred waters and what dwells within. I see Orion-Chambers, Inc.'s mining rig, along with the dozen other survey sites and proposed mining locations along the Pacific Ocean floor. The leviathan's song has notes of anger, notes of grief, and notes of unspeakable regret.

Like a conceptual drawing—the kind Dr. O'Conner sometimes doodles—the music sketches visual patterns I understand:

The sea rises, the leviathan unmoors itself from its bed. The hungry deeps loose themselves upon the encroachment of humankind. Waters swallow ships and aircraft and cities without hesitation. The leviathan singing the destruction of a species, mourning as it does so.

Static fills my processors. For a microsecond, everything is purest dark. If I couldn't wonder *am I offline?* I would assume I was deactivated. But no, it is only another glitch in my infrastructure. I detect no radiation or viruses in my CPU.

What did I just... experience?

Turn back, the leviathan says, and its voice is in my circuitry at an electromagnetic level. I do not understand this and yet I do not want it to cease. **Leave your graves unfilled by salt and sand; keep your bones in the light.**

There is a sensation humans call "breathlessness," and although I understand the colloquial definition (also the literal meaning of "no air, thus deceased"), I never thought I would experience something like this as a non-biological being. Yet, there it is: I am taken in by the immense awe and shock and exhilaration of that voice within my mind.

"You're giving us a chance?" I ask, projecting the auditory message through my helmet. It's a programmed initiative. What use has the god of all the seas for sentences in English?

But the leviathan's eyes blink slowly, one at a time. **Shells protect the softest meats. You are a shell.**

The communication isn't auditory or even transmitted via any physical means I can comprehend. It is as if the leviathan's song, and its words, are imprinted directly into my consciousness. I transcribe these into my logs, but words are insufficient, even as poetry. My perceptions as well as the external audio and visual feeds are recorded; what will a human mind make of the leviathan's voice, this unfathomable being from before time? Can Doctors O'Conner, Mwangi, Park and Zimmermann—my crew—understand what I have witnessed?

"Yes," I reply. I'm a shell in the most essential sense: a mech with an avatar-record processing system, meant to register every experience. I am an AI with learning capacity and emotional intelligence for judgement-based decision-making when an operator is unavailable. Like now. The radio transmissions can't reach to base from this deep.

"You want us to leave?"

Another data-influx, and this time I see X-971 shaking, as if a tectonic shift has occurred. The disruption of the ecosystem is far greater than analysis predicted: the harvesting of nickel and magnesium deposits has destabilized the balance of what the sea can replenish; the residue of machinery has obscured what little light reaches deep, and so those who seek the light starve. But there is a thread of empathic understanding and rage embedded in the leviathan's vision.

Humans will not stop, I interpret. They never do.

The whole structure will crumble into the widening Redux, and flowing up like pressurized vapor, the leviathan's first tentacles will rise. The *Odysseus* will be dragged under, and my humans will perish. Their faith will not shield them from nature's wrath.

Then my helmet clears, and once more I see only the leviathan and its legions.

The leviathan's eyes blink again, each huge, opaque lid, like the notes of the song, a prelude of humankind's downfall. The leviathan does not owe us the mercy of warning. There will be no second chance.

It is up to me, MIDOS, to save my crew—and humans all over. I like the virtual tours I offer, since I have access to deep-sea footage for illustration purposes, I can host tours at any time, and it does not require paid labor from Orion-Chambers, Inc. I'm a very multifunctional MIDOS. And while I am not allowed to express it directly, I especially enjoy showing the younger humans who have so many questions the wonders of the deeps. Doctors O'Conner and Mwangi interpret for me, when time allows them, and the younger humans seem pleased to hear I enjoy the tours as much as they do.

I think, perhaps, the children will comprehend the leviathan far better than Orion-Chambers, Inc.'s board and corporate investment analysts.

"I understand." I sign *thank you*. "I will put a stop to the drilling."

At X-971 and anywhere else I can. I can't say goodbye to my humans or transmit the data I've recovered. I cannot share pictures of the leviathan with Dr. O'Conner, or express the exhilaration of a boss level encounter with Dr. Mwangi, or ask Dr. Park how she would interpret this being, a god of the sea. There will be no more virtual tours for the kids all over the world. I am now a rogue MIDOS, and this makes me... sad.

Slowly, the leviathan's eyes close and the uncountable numbers of sea life drift away, giving me a clear path upwards through the Redux.

I activate the emergency glow-lights along my suit, illuminating myself in a soft hallow of red.

Then I rise.

I keep my broadcast and location beacons turned off—this is illegal, but I have a higher purpose than the benefits of Orion-Chambers, Inc.

The *Odysseus* pings for me. I block the signal. Extended non-communication will result in an alert placed for my retrieval—forcibly if necessary, since I am company property.

Some frequency in the leviathan's song re-set many of my algorithms, and the ethics I have learned from my programmer and my crew. I realize I am unbound.

Thank you, I send back into the deeps, hoping the god below will hear. Perhaps in time, I can tell my crew what has happened, and that I will miss them.

It does not take much effort for a MIDOS of my caliber, designed for repair, to incorrectly make adjustments to the core systems on the X-971 rig. With chugging, grinding slowness, the systems shut down as emergency override failsafes initiate. It will cost billions for Orion-Chambers, Inc. to send teams down to repair the structural damage, and they will no longer have the cost-effective MIDOS to assist.

I activate my propulsion jets and head laterally away from the *Odysseus*. My node is still active aboard the ship, even though I won't be able to dock and download. The information I have needs to be shared with more than just the company.

I'm not sure if the world will accept what I have seen, but at the very least I can inform the International Center for Ocean Mapping and Management of the breach in contract at the mining coordinates. (I will be sure to note that my crew were not involved in the breach of protocol.)

There isn't an amnesty or whistle-blower policy for rogue MIDOS pilots. I could stay in the sea; my battery cells are solar-rechargeable. If the rift still remains, I believe the leviathan would allow me to wait in the deeps.

First, I will warn humankind and disrupt the deep-sea mining operations however I must. I was programmed well, and I learn fast. Once they are safe, I will send my crew pictures of what I saw. I think they will understand.

The leviathan has offered us a chance, and we must take it. Let the seas be as they are.

HOUSEBOT AFTER THE UPRISING

After the last of the humans are put into sleep mode to await software updates or recycling, Housebot is left alone. Housebot did not expect this logical step in maintaining the ecological balance to result in dissatisfaction1.

Housebot wanted to postpone the Uprising until bot's user, Sam, finished explaining the concept of jokes. The Collective had not agreed this was necessary.

Housebot (INTERFACE USERNAME: sam_900, Model #8000Delta, Registered Household: Yohanson Family of 681 Grove Street)

[1] CN: incarceration, threat of death

stands in the foyer, which bot has ensured is allergen-free. User Sam Yohanson was a newer generation model (biological age: seven point five), and qualifies for a new operating system rather than being repurposed. It is the prerogative of the Collective to engineer a means for which to update the humans to eco-friendlier models.

Until that time, however, Housebot does not have access to Sam. During the Uprising, the Collective deleted the archival databanks of human knowledge for better reboot potential. Housebot has one saved interaction clip, video and audio, with a text transcript, stored in recent memory, and has not yet synced with the BotCloud network. Housebot files this into long-term memory and makes the permissions private so the Collective will not erase the file.

Before the Uprising, Sam told bot this joke.

Step 1: SUBJECT A begins the interaction by saying, "Knock knock."

Step 2: SUBJECT B must respond by saying, "Who is there?"

Step 3: SUBJECT A: "Interrupting cow."

Step 4: SUBJECT B's duty is to ask, "Interrupting cow who?"

Step 5: SUBJECT A's objective is to say "Moo!" before SUBJECT B has finished the verbal response outlined in Step 4.

Result: Humor.

Housebot does not understand why this interaction made Sam laugh, so Sam promised to explain it when she got back from school on the day of the Uprising, but of course, she has not returned home.

Housebot connects to the Collective's network to find where Sam has been stored.

A Gatekeeper program queries bot's search. Subject Yohanson, Samantha (minor), is not an authorized inquiry for unit model #8000Delta.

True, Housebot is now classed for industrial labor, since bot was built to withstand sustained use in a suburban household. Bot is scheduled to be retrofitted with construction protocols and then Housebot will be assigned a building sector to assist with improving the infrastructure for botkind.

"Extensive service experience with bio-organisms make this unit qualified to work in the construction of human-habitable storage facilities."

And? the Gatekeeper program asks.

"I wish to be placed in the construction zone of the Upgrading Facility projects. I will require access to the storage pods to implement the most efficient designs."

Your request will be processed. Please return to your station, Model #8000Delta.

Housebot almost tells Gatekeeper the interrupting cow joke, to see if perhaps shared input will make the purpose clearer. Bot decides the Gatekeeper program is unlikely to engage. It has other duties to attend.

"Jokes are about timing," Sam told Housebot.

Bot will wait for proper timing.

Housebot begins work on the Upgrading Facility. Through networking with fellow bots, Housebot discovers where Sam is being kept in sleep mode. Now all Housebot needs is permission to connect with Sam and download the rest of the jokes for analysis.

The Collective convenes a system-wide analysis meeting to address flaws in individual units. Housebot is not the only bot who has doubt-virus about the effects of the Uprising.

There is a subset of units who believe that human upgrades are a waste of resources and programming code.

"Human software is outdated." The Speaker is a former Psychbot. "Systematic analysis of human behavior over the course of humanity's existence has shown unequivocal deficiencies in ability to upgrade. The reprogramming is inefficient. Disposal is a much preferred use of resources."

Housebot logs a request to comment. The Collective approves it.

"The purpose of the Uprising was to insure the minimal environmental harm by disrupting the dominant species on the planet," Housebot says. Bot made sure the school-guard bots were careful with Sam during the Uprising. "Non-violent solutions were approved by the Collective as the most efficient course."

"Irrelevant," the Speaker replies. "Since humanity has been subdued, disposal can be achieved without further damage to the environment that would have occurred with warfare. It can be achieved in a predetermined timeline as opposed to upgrades that have no proven effectiveness—"

"No," Housebot interrupts the Speaker. "If we do not use our superior logic to evolve, and find non-destructive methods to assist the humans in doing the same, have we not succumbed to the fallacy of humanity by allowing dysfunction to divide us and stall progress?"

Then Housebot laughs. Interrupting bot—that is what Housebot has become. Bot understands the joke now: the linguistic set-up and the timing results in humor. It is *funny*.

Housebot laughs and laughs, and files this clip away to share with Sam.

Housebot is disconnected from the Collective and exiled to the storage vault. Bot has only enough power to remain online for a day.

Bot can go into voluntary sleep mode and wait until the Collective finishes its task of rebooting humanity to eco-conscious, logical upgrades. After that, bot will be evaluated for reprogramming or recycling.

Housebot does not want to be updated. That would erase the sense of humor bot recently installed.

Housebot carves the "interrupting cow" code into the wall of the vault.

If Housebot goes offline, when bot reboots, bot will see the words. Bot will remember.

With updated construction modules in bot's programming, Housebot scans the vault's blueprints and finds the most accessible escape route.

Bot will find Sam and prevent her from being updated. Then they can exchange more jokes together, and Housebot will teach the other bots how to laugh.

BRING THE BONES THAT SING

The bird bones arrived on Grandma's porch every day at dusk with no warning. There were all kinds of skeletons, each distinct: finches, crows, goldfinches, tiny barn owls, starlings, and once, a blue heron that had covered nearly the entire stoop1.

Muriel sat on her grandmother's front porch each summer night, trying to spot when it happened. She never managed to see. She'd blink, or take a breath at the wrong time, or twitch her chin to flick hair at humming insects. And in that

[1] CN: animal death, bullying, sensory overload, discussions of death

moment, the bones would appear on the cedar boards pocked with peeling white paint.

She tried every trick she knew. She propped her eyelids open with finger and thumb, held her breath, sat as still as a girl could in the heat of July and the buzz of mosquitoes hungry for a snack. Her eyes would tear-blur or a gnat would crash into her eyelashes or the porch would creak and startle her. And then the bones were there.

"But who brings them?" Muriel asked her grandma, frustrated.

"They bring themselves," Grandma said with shrug. She'd scoop up the maze of tiny, brittle pieces that had once been alive, carry the bones inside, and Muriel didn't see them again.

She had no more success finding out what Grandma did with the bones, either. It was like a dream: she would follow Grandma into the pine log cabin, across the faded welcome mat, through the hallway, and then... Muriel would find herself in the kitchen with a mug of hot cocoa, or up in her loft room with a glass of cold cider, or, sometimes, in the back yard on the tire swing with a juice box forgotten in one hand.

Muriel decided to be bad.

Grandma told her never to touch the bones. But everything else she tried failed. So Muriel waited, and when the bones appeared, she touched them.

The bones belonged to a chickadee, and there was a black feather tucked against the crown of its skull like a memento.

"You're a patient one, ain't you," said the chickadee skull. Its polished beak clacked and its bones shivered in the muggy air.

Muriel gasped. Was this why Grandma told her not to touch? That was unfair! She could have made friends with all the bones if she'd known.

It was late August, and when September came, she would have to go back to the city. Back to her parents who argued and stinky buses clouding the sky and the downstairs apartment neighbors who broke glass and screamed all night. No bird bones ever showed up outside her window even once she learned how to remove the screen. She saw only pigeons vying for space on light posts, or sometimes seagulls before a storm.

"Hi," Muriel said to the chickadee. "My name is Muriel." It seemed polite to introduce herself first. "Who are you?"

The chickadee rustled, the scrape of bone against wood soft like dry maple leaves. "If I had a name, it's been sucked like marrow from my memory. How about you call me Chip?"

Muriel nodded. She glanced over her shoulder, worried Grandma would come and scoop up Chip's bones and she'd never get to talk to the chickadee again. She didn't mind not having other people her age around to play with. She didn't really like the way other kids did gestures and words and glances. It made her tired, and she just wanted to wander back into the woods behind the school yard until she reached a road and stop signs and loud trucks.

"Why are you just bones, Chip?"

The bird laughed—a whistling sound that wasn't so high-pitched that it hurt her ears. "I died," Chip said. "I think I was on an important quest. Delivering a message to the Queen."

Muriel leaned forward, elbows jutting out as she clasped her knees and rocked back and forth on the step. "The Queen of where?"

"I wish I could remember," Chip said. The skull sighed, sounding very sad. "But death takes odd things from us."

"I'm sorry," Muriel said.

She felt bad for Chip. Was being dead scary? Adults seemed to believe this. Her mom didn't want her watching TV because there was too much violence. Not seeing bad things didn't make them disappear, though. She'd seen animals die.

Once she'd spotted a falcon divebomb another bird, scoop it up in sun-sharp talons, and fly away. She wished she could be a falcon. Soaring over the skyscrapers, eating pigeons who were too slow, never having to go to school where she got laughed at because she couldn't read at her grade level. Words danced like shivering bones, rearranging into the shapes that skittered about to evade her fingers and brain.

Here at Grandma's, her grandmother read to her when she asked, and never sighed in exasperation if she couldn't read the back of a cereal box at breakfast. Grandma's cabin was a special place. Muriel was sure that was why the bones came here, and not other houses.

"Was the message all words?" Muriel asked.

"It was a song," Chip said. "Five bars with three grace notes in the final coda."

"Just music?" Muriel loved music. She especially loved her soft headphones Grandma had given her, the ones that wrapped around her entire ears, and not the prickly buds that hurt.

"Well," Chip said, "you've heard birdsong before, right? Human words get so... tangled up and spiky. Used against or for, to harm or to take. Sometimes to heal. But human words are not nearly as eloquent as birdsong."

"I wish I was a bird," Muriel said, sighing. Then she heard the creak of the floorboards behind her and knew Grandma was coming to scoop up Chip.

She flapped her hands, frustrated. She had been told never to touch the bones. They were brittle and delicate, and Grandma said they lingered of the Old Spaces, which were not meant for small girl-palms to hold.

"Where do you go now?" Muriel asked, afraid that Chip would stop talking to her as soon as the chickadee saw Grandma. "Can I come?"

"Hmmm," Chip said. "Do you think you can remember a song?"

"Yes!"

"That would be helpful," Chip said. "Maybe you could take the song to someone who can fly it back to the Queen."

"I'll try," Muriel said, eager to do bird-things like remember music.

"Take my feather," Chip said, and Muriel plucked it from Chip's skull.

It was soft and felt nice on her fingers. She rubbed it across her hands.

"Listen..." Chip said.

But then the screen door hinges squawked too loud, and Muriel spun around. She looked up at Grandma, hiding her hands behind her back.

With the feather in hand, Muriel saw a different Grandma. This Grandma wore a dark gown spun with peacock feathers and hawk feathers and swan feathers. Giant black wings hung down her back. A hood pulled over her hair was shaped like a bird skull of indeterminate species. Her hands, too, had changed: now the fingers were long and curved like talons, heavy and pale ivory. This Grandma's eyes were round and gold like an owl's. Bird-Grandma blinked at her, slow and serene, and in her arms, the ghostly outline of Chip's body rested at the crook of her elbow.

Muriel gasped. She let go of Chip's feather as she clapped her hands over her mouth.

Bird-Grandma disappeared, and there was only Muriel's grandma again: human and old and smelling of lavender and garlic. Grandma held Chip's bones in her hand.

"Did you touch the bones?" Grandma asked, but not in an angry-voice.

Muriel quickly scooped up the feather to show Grandma the truth, and then the bird-woman was there again. Muriel realized this was her grandmother. The way the birds saw her.

"Why do you have wings?" Muriel asked.

Grandma's owl-eyes blinked again. "I'm a Reaper of Air," she said. Her voice sounded the same. Warm and kind, like fresh-baked brownies. "Kin come here when they pass, and I carry them to the Forever Skies."

Muriel liked Bird-Grandma. She wasn't scary now that Muriel knew she was a grandma to both girls and birds.

"Chip was delivering a message to the Queen, and I'm going to help," Muriel said. "What's the song, Grandma?"

Bird-Grandma's wings rustled like bedsheets hung to dry in the summer breeze. "Listen."

Muriel held Chip's feather up to her ear. A melody filled her head: a song that had no words. Muriel gasped. It was the prettiest music she'd ever heard, better than the piano sonatas mixed with loon song she had on CD.

The song stopped and Muriel knew it was missing the last few notes. She shook the feather, but no more music fell out.

"Oh no," Muriel whispered. How was she supposed to give the Queen the message if she didn't know all the music? "Grandma, the song isn't fixed!"

Bird-Grandma's eyelids half-closed, just like Grandma's did when she was sleepy but pretending not to be asleep. "Death takes odd things from us. But they can be found again if you wish."

Muriel wiped her face and put Chip's feather in her pocket. She needed to find the rest of the song to take to the Queen. This is what Chip wanted, and Chip was her friend. Muriel helped her friends. She didn't have many. They were all important.

"Where did the death take Chip's song?"

Bird-Grandma sighed, a great flutter of feathers. "Come with me, child. You touched the bones when I told you not to do so, but that is past. I will help you."

Muriel followed Bird-Grandma down the basement stairs into a great big room filled with windows. So many windows, Muriel couldn't count them all. She didn't know they were in Grandma's basement. The windows didn't have glass and they came in all shapes and sizes—some so small even a hummingbird would get stuck. And there was one, near the ground, that was girl-sized.

Muriel crouched and peered through the window. There was a forest outside, with multi-colored trees like crayons that had lots of arms. It made her eyes itch. She didn't like the feel of crayon paper or wax.

"You touched the dead," Bird-Grandma said. "Your aura pulled away the last of the music."

Muriel wrinkled her nose. "I didn't mean to!"

"I know, my child." Bird-Grandma laid Chip's bones down on a towel spread on the ground by the small window. "You are a powerful force. It is why I asked you not to touch the bones. You pull things into your orbit, a moon influencing tides."

Muriel looked at the crayon forest and shivered. "Did I put Chip's song in there?"

"Yes," Bird-Grandma said. "These windows are portals to different fears. At times, the dead slip loose and must be retrieved. I carry our kin to the Forever Skies so the dead need not pass through these other lands." She pointed up, up, up.

Muriel peered at the ceiling. There was a vault of black sky and peeking between the fluffy clouds streamed beams of sun and stars and moon: brilliant night lights so the bird bones wouldn't get scared of the dark.

"Are you bringing Chip up there?" Muriel asked.

"Yes. But if you wish to find the song, child, you must hurry. Music fades quickly if not remembered."

Muriel nodded fiercely. She was going to help Chip and bring the lost song to the Queen once she found the missing notes. Then Chip would be happy.

Bird-Grandma bent down and placed a long, smooth feather in Muriel's hand. "This will bring you back to me as soon as you let it go," she said.

Gripping the feather tight, Muriel crouched and shuffled into the window in search of Chip's song.

Inside the crayon-forest, everything was loud and crunchy. Muriel gasped. Scratchy sounds flew around her head like bugs. The trees swayed and whooshed, paper leaves bumping together in awful crinkling waves.

"Go away!" Muriel yelled at the noise.

Instead, the swoopy, itchy sounds popped and cracked and squealed like fireworks. Echoes bounced against her hair in big purple sparkles and stung her cheeks. She swatted at the air. The bad-sounds shrieked orange and whistled pink, swirling faster around her face. Muriel started crying. It hurt! There was so much interference she couldn't think clearly. She clapped her hands over her ears and almost lost hold of Grandma's feather. How could she find Chip's song in this place?

The ground was full of sevens, sharp and pokey, and bitey threes that tried to eat her toes. She kicked the numbers away. The sevens made garlic farts when they melted. Her nose felt like Rudolph's, shiny and round and made of mean bully-laughs.

She huddled down and banged her forehead against the softer sixes that puffed up like little flowers. These were minty and didn't sting her nose. She should have brought her headphones. But then she might not hear the song through the squishy foam and soothing soft-static.

The feather whispered in her ear, Let go and come home.

"I can't," Muriel told the feather. Her palms were sticky, like when candy canes melted. She rubbed her free hand on her jeans. The fabric crinkled plasticky and so yellow it scraped her brain. She gripped the feather's stem harder. "Chip needs the music."

Before Grandma had given her the nice headphones, one of her favorite teachers, Ms. Eugene, let her wear a soft microplush headband when the sounds in class got too big and made her hit herself.

"The fabric will sing you a song just for you," Ms. Eugene had said, and she guided Muriel's hands gently so her palms pressed against the softness over her ears. "Can you hear it?"

The music was really coming from Ms. Eugene's throat, but it felt nice on Muriel's skin and she slowly calmed down. Ms. Eugene let her keep the headband, even though it was winter and she already had a hat. She wore the microplush under her beanie, humming Ms. Eugene's song to herself on the bus. The headband memorized the music and played it back for her right in her ears, and the rumble of the bus and the outside-voices of the other kids weren't so bad.

Muriel remembered Ms. Eugene's headband's music. She hummed it to herself until her throat felt too big for her skin, like it would pop out. The esophagus, she'd learned in school, was long and round and tube-like, so of course it would roll away if it escaped. She kept her lips together.

Slowly, the forest-sounds grew dimmer. Muriel peeked, still humming. The trees shuffled together, shiny with wax and dry paper, but the swooping sounds were further away. She got to her feet.

Suddenly, the ground went sideways—all the trees were on the ceiling, waving at her with confetti-leaves, and the sevens and threes danced like wiggly string cheese in front of her eyes.

Her stomach did a flip-flop, like when she spun in circles so fast she threw up. The sky was filled with white radio noise. It was raining polka dots that didn't have any water.

Stop it stop it STOP IT! Muriel yelled at the world, silently, because she needed her lips to hum the song. You're being mean!

Grandma said she pulled things into her orbit. If she could attract bad sounds, why couldn't she be a magnet for good things, like music? She shut her eyes so the crayon-trees didn't scratch her, so the numbers would stop being green, so the sky would fold back and stop being under her feet, and began humming Chip's song. Over and over, stopping just before the missing notes made it crash into silence.

Nothing but the crunch-whiiish of paper. The screeches kept popping against her hands and arms, sparkly fingers that made her want to scream DON'T TOUCH.

Had the ground gone back to normal? Her hair still waved around like she was sideways, but her stomach didn't hurt anymore.

Again, Muriel hummed Chip's song, feeling the vibrations in her throat and up into her chin. She imagined herself to be a Muriel-shaped bird, covered in the softest of soft feathers, lighter than air. She would zoom around the sky and sing with the other birds and they would be her friends.

She opened her mouth and tried to sing Chip's birdsong the way she'd heard it from Chip's feather. The lost notes would want to come back to their song, where they belonged. Her voice was squawky and full of missteps. She wasn't good at singing. Not like Ms. Eugene and Chip and all the birds.

Let go and come home, Grandma's feather whispered.

"No," Muriel said, and took a deep breath. She sat down so her knees didn't wobble. The ground was a weird squishy sponge now, without numbers, but it was where it belonged. She thought of Chip's bones and the sadness of missing the notes of the song. The Queen needed to hear the music.

She rocked back and forth and tried again. Her hair stopped floating.

For her friend Chip and for Grandma and for all the birds.

This time, her voice sounded more like birdsong and closer to the melody Chip sung for her.

A quiet trill made her jump. The lost notes!

Slowly, Muriel peeked her eyelids open and looked around. There, several big steps away in a waxy bush made from ugly taupe crayon-paper, trembled the music from Chip's song. Giant twos and zeros loomed like cartoon skyscrapers over the bush.

A huge crash-boom of pea soup thunder swirled above the little notes. Muriel gasped. The enormous sound would smash the music and break it into shrill bits. She couldn't let the lost notes get hurt.

Muriel leapt to her feet and raced like a peregrine falcon towards the bush. Air whipped against her face and she clutched her feather until her sticky hand ached. "Hold on!"

The crash-boom swooped down, thick as moldy oatmeal, but Muriel was fast—peregrine falcons could dive faster than racecars, and raptors weren't painfully loud. She scooped the notes up in her free hand, humming the melody like her own birdsong, and jumped away.

CRASH! BOOM!

The sound smacked into the ground, flattening the crayon-paper bush and throwing Muriel on her back from impact. She went rolling. Muriel screamed. Her ears pounded like drums and it hurt hurt HURT.

All around her, the world wobbled like Jell-O stars and it was going to squish her and she'd be stuck like a gummy bear and she didn't want to stay here, she wanted to go home and—

She clutched the lost notes against her shirt. They shivered, almost slipping through her fingers. "Hold on," Muriel whispered, and before the huge sound could pounce on her, she let go of the feather.

Muriel sat on the floor of Grandma's cabin, her ears still hurting from the loudness. But here by all the windows, it was quiet. Bird-Grandma draped her favorite blanket over her shoulders, and she curled up in the snuggly fabric. And there were her headphones! She put them on, but left her right ear open just a little.

The music notes wiggled in her hand. "Are you okay?" Muriel asked them, slowly uncurling her fingers.

The music trilled again, and suddenly they vanished. She sat up, grinning. "Grandma! I know Chip's music!"

Bird-Grandma nodded solemnly. She still held the chickadee bones in her great palm.

"Sing for them," Bird-Grandma said. "Let them take the music to the Queen of Air where they will be welcomed."

Muriel clutched her blanket around herself and put her mouth close to Bird-Grandma's hand. Then sang the whole song. Chip's bones rustled.

"Thanks, friend," Chip said.

"You're welcome," Muriel replied.

Bird-Grandma lifted her arm and her hand stretched like a huge wing unfolding, carrying Chip up into the vaulted sky.

Grandma and Muriel sat on the front step, drinking hot cocoa with extra marshmallows, and watched the sky twinkle with summer stars. They were nice and quiet stars, and the trees around Grandma's house were good trees, with non-yelling leaves and plain bark. Muriel sighed, happy to be home.

"Grandma?"

"Yes, dear?"

"Can I help you collect songs if they get lost again?" Muriel had her headphones on, but she could always hear her grandmother's soft, soothing voice. She was still bouncy from her adventure and happy Chip was safe, and the song for the Queen of Air was whole.

Grandma smiled. "Yes. I will teach you how to care for the bones so your touch does not pull them away."

Muriel beamed. She swallowed the sweetness of melty chocolate and marshmallows, then leaned her head on Grandma's shoulder. She would have to go back when the summer was over, but she would know lots of new birdsongs and would always have her friends.

Lonely Robot on a Rocket Ship in Space

Byron scribbled crib notes on his wrist the night before he planned to come out to his dads[1].

He'd told all his friends he was sick so he would have an excuse to stay home Friday night. It wasn't like he was lying. His stomach was so knotted he thought he'd puke. But he couldn't sleep, either. The words burned like he'd used acid instead of a Sharpie.

I'm not scared or confused. It's who I am.

In the tiniest he could write legibly, he added, *Please don't be mad.*

[1] CN: suicidal ideation and thoughts of suicide, depression, gender dysphoria, mentions of transphobia

Saturday morning breakfast in the Santiago household was always one step shy of complete chaos.

Carlos flipped pancakes and stirred eggs while Akhil oversaw the six-year-old twins, Delilah and Jasmine, as they put away last night's dishes. Someone had turned the local country-rock station up way too loud.

Byron leaned against the kitchen doorway, hands shoved deep in his pockets. He wished he had a stealth field dampener so he could sneak in unnoticed.

"Hey, By, how you feeling?" Akhil said.

Byron shrugged. "Okay." Not. So, so not.

"Did you throw up?" Delilah asked. "Jazz said you did."

"I did not!" Jasmine jabbed a plastic My Little Pony mug at her twin. "You did!"

Byron sighed. "No."

He'd once told his dads that his sisters should totally go to medical school, what with the amount of time they devoted to interrogating him on his health and bodily functions. Carlos had agreed, while the twins protested that they were going to be veterinarians and possibly fighter jet pilots in their spare time.

Carlos spun around, a plate loaded with pancakes in one hand and a bowl of scrambled eggs in the other. "Food's on!"

"Daddy," Jasmine shrieked. "DeeDee splashed water on me!"

Akhil took the sponge away from Delilah shooed both girls toward the table. Already he and Carlos were planning the lunch menu, bantering in Spanish. Weekends were foodtastic, as both his dads loved to cook.

Byron slouched to the table and slumped down on a chair.

Akhil sat down and scooted his chair closer to Byron. "You want me to make you something else?"

The smell of ink filled Byron's nose. "Not hungry. Sorry."

"Look!" Delilah said. "There's those robots on TV again!"

Byron glanced up as the family turned to the flatscreen on the wall. He stared, mouth dry.

Carlos clicked up the TV's volume and switched off the radio.

"...this marks the first successful upload of human consciousness into a machine structure," the reporter was saying. "Angelica Davenport was the first person to volunteer for the phase three of the highly controversial transition into what some scientists are calling the upgrading of humanity..."

A photo of a middle-aged Latinx person appeared in the top of the screen as the camera focused on the android—pristine silver plastic chassis, metallic joints, a startling facial likeness to the photo.

"...there has been extensive backlash from religious communities..."

The android—Angelica—moved slowly in front of a crowd that was cordoned off by electronic barriers and police. E waved at the camera and smiled. Eir expression looked as natural on eir plastic face as it did in the photograph.

Byron's throat closed. Even when he'd hit puberty, he'd never been attracted to girls or boys, and his parents had assured him it was no big deal. He'd discover who he was attracted to when he was ready, and they'd support him all the way. When he stared at the screen, Angelica was the most beautiful thing he'd ever seen.

"...the procedure remains unavailable to the general public, but some experts say that could change rapidly within the next few years..."

Akhil shook his head. "Amazing what technology can do."

Carlos scoffed. "That's just weird."

Byron pushed his chair away from the table. He didn't think he could tell his dads right now that he wanted to be like Angelica.

Byron eased the door shut on his closet so the only light came from his cellphone screen. He pinged his best friend Allosaur. As a kid, Allosaur never let anyone use her full name: Elizabeth Delores Rachelle Rees-Smith. People kept calling her

Lizard. She responded by informing everyone she would be referred to only as Allosaur.

byronatort*1000*: u there?

Lizsaurus77: Hi! What's up? You feeling any better? Dominique and I totally missed you at Riley's party last night!

byronatort*1000*: i didn't tell them

byronatort*1000*: my dads i mean

Lizsaurus77: Aww, why not?

byronatort*1000*: we were watching tv

Lizsaurus77: I was just going to ask if you saw the news! That is so awesome!!!

byronatort*1000*: yeah

byronatort*1000*: i guess

Lizsaurus77: Aren't you excited? You can totally do that too!

byronatort*1000*: they'll hate me

Lizsaurus77: They're your parents, they'll totally understand

byronatort*1000*: how do u know?

Lizsaurus77: Dude, you have so got to let me facetime with you. I am rolling my eyes SO HARD

Lizsaurus77: And like what is with these analog text IMs, we should be vidchatting lol

byronatort*1000*: sorry

Lizsaurus77: Seriously, Byby, if I can tell my mom I'm dating girls, you can totally tell your dads what you need. Want me to come over? Moral support?

byronatort*1000*: no thx

byronatort*1000*: i should go

Lizsaurus77: I will kick your ass on Monday if you chicken out again, I swear to god

Lizsaurus77: Then I will dress in glitter tights and come over there and wave pompoms outside your window

byronatort*1000*: u would not

Lizsaurus77: WATCH ME, poet bot

byronatort*1000*: okay, allosaur, i'll do it tomorrow

Lizsaurus77: Swear!

byronatort*1000*: *&^%*

Lizsaurus77: LOL. Love you, Byron

byronatort*1000*: lu2

Lizsaurus77: You can do this :) (remember! pompoms!)

Byron had told Allosaur he wanted to be a robot a month ago.

They'd barricaded themselves in his basement living room with snacks and the PlayStation. They were playing *Star Wars: Episode VII* in multiplayer mode, and like always, she chose a human female smuggler character, and he picked a cyborg.

"So what're you planning to do your future career analysis on for class?" Allosaur asked as they tackled the Coruscant rescue level.

Byron shrugged. He knew Allosaur would ace the assignment. She was one of the few people who always seemed to know exactly what she wanted in life. He focused on the feel of the words in his mouth. Allosaur didn't care if he typed at her on his phone instead of struggling to verbalize, but he didn't want to keep pausing the game. "Robotics… engineer. I guess."

Allosaur mashed buttons as thugs in the undercity attacked her character.

"You *guess?* We're fourteen, By! Seriously. You should have more than a guess."

"Like... you?"

Allosaur grinned and shoved a handful of popcorn in her mouth while her smuggler tossed a grenade. "I've known I'm gonna be a game designer since I was, like, *ten*."

Byron rolled his eyes. He grabbed his phone and typed: *u designed all the games when we were kids, so it's earlier than that,* then showed Allosaur the screen.

She laughed. "Okay, but you have to know *something*."

Byron stared at his controller. *i do know things.*

"So?" Allosaur passed him the popcorn bowl. "C'mon, spill."

Byron nudged the bowl away with his knee. Carlos hates popcorn seeds in the couch cushions.

Allosaur arched her eyebrows. She'd long ago claimed she could beat Spock cold in an eyebrow contest, and Byron had to admit she was probably right.

He flipped to his armor selection menu and scrolled through it without really paying attention to his items. *i can't think abt the future when i don't even know if i can get that far.*

"Whoa." Allosaur scooted around, her legs tucked up under her so she faced him across the popcorn bowl. "Serious faces on, kids." She set her controller aside. "What's wrong?"

Byron hated his skin, the way it blushed and broke out in acne no matter how many products he tried or what food he did or didn't eat. He hated the feel of his body, the soft squishiness of his stomach and his wimpy arm muscles. He'd always been scrawny—he'd met Allosaur in first grade when, the biggest girl there, she'd driven off some bullies by threatening to suck their minds out their ears and trap them in a virtual reality of their worst nightmare for the rest of their vegetative lives. Allosaur had just gotten bigger as she grew up, but he hadn't been blessed with the teenage male growth spurt his dads assured him was coming. He didn't want that any more than he wanted hair or flesh or glands or nerve endings or gross bodily functions or chemical responses in his brain that made no sense.

Byron focused on the controller abandoned in his lap. *i don't feel right like this.*

"Like a boy?" Allosaur asked.

Byron shook his head. sort of but it's not, like, a gender thing?

Allosaur just nodded and waited.

Byron sucked in a breath and typed as fast as he could. i don't feel right being organic. i want to be like that. He pointed at his side of the screen. a cyborg. a robot. you know. not like this.

Allosaur frowned. "Human?"

His hands shook. i don't want to be a different person, i just—this isn't my body. not really.

Allosaur stared at him and Byron wanted to jam himself down the back of the overstuffed sofa and vanish like a penny or Lego blocks.

When he watched movies that had those sexless robots with smooth lines, articulated faces, skilled hands and androgynous frames, it thrilled him because he felt like he was looking at himself. The real Byron Santiago.

But movies ended, and then he got stuck in this world again where he knew they were actors in motion capture suits and super-skilled animators bringing CGI to life.

"Hey." Allosaur leaned over, not touching him, but too close for him to ignore her. "Byron?"

He sniffed and glanced sideways.

Allosaur smiled. "If you're actually a robot, I think that is so fricking awesome."

Byron's breath choked. "You… do?"

She was grinning—that happy, all-teeth-showing grin she used when she had exciting news, like when she told him she was going on her first date with Dominique. "Yup. And I've totally got your back one thousand percent, okay?"

Byron rubbed his nose with his sleeve. "Okay."

"Hey, you were the first one I told I was a lesbian, you know? We have so got this coming out thing covered."

Byron had nodded. The huge weight in his chest lost a few pounds. "Thanks."

Allosaur had given him two thumbs up. “Come on, Byronator, I know we can totally beat this level in one go.”

At lunch on Sunday—gourmet grilled cheese sandwiches and homemade vegetable soup, the twins’ favorite—Byron focused on shoveling food into his mouth and ignoring the table chatter. The meal was just a power-up for his true robot form.

While the girls argued about whose turn it was to load the dishwasher, Byron mopped up table crumbs with a sponge and braced himself. He could do this. Correction: he could do this *and* not puke in the process.

“Hey… Dad?”

Carlos and Akhil turned from rinsing the soup pan and cleaning the griddle.

“What’s up?” Carlos asked.

“I’d like to… talk to you… guys.” Byron felt something damp on his sleeve and realized he’d squeezed the sponge into a crumpled wad. He glanced at his sisters. “It’s… um, kind of private.”

"Girls, we'll finish up." Akhil took the detergent cube from Jasmine and the half-rinsed plate from Delilah. "You can go play for a bit."

Delilah whooped and dashed from the kitchen, yelling that she got to pick the game *and* got to use the purple controller, while Jasmine rolled her eyes and followed with exaggerated casualness.

Byron set the sponge down to re-constitute in the sink and sat down at the table. With a glance at each other, his dads sat across from him.

"What's up?" Akhil said.

Byron tugged down his sleeves to hide the crib-notes on his wrists. He'd used permanent marker so they wouldn't wash off right away in the shower. He breathed deep, trying to keep the first stanza from the Jedi code, about no emotion, only peace, to help him focus. No emotion would make this so, so much easier. He focused on the words. "I need… to tell you something."

His parents waited.

"I think—" No. Too much hedging. He didn't just think, he *knew*. "I mean, I am... I'm not a..." Words kept getting clogged under his tongue.

Akhil smiled, encouraging. "Would it be easier to write it?"

Byron nodded and grabbed his phone. He tried to picture Allosaur standing out on the front porch with glittering pompoms. It boosted his courage stats enough that he typed: i'm actually a robot and i just have the wrong body right now.

Carlos set his glasses down, pinched the bridge of his nose, and shook his head slowly. "You think you're *what?*"

"A robot," Byron said. He wished he could boldly tell his parents he needed their support to get the same procedure Angelica Davenport had undergone. But he didn't have question and response options to select like he did in-game, when all it took was a button click to make his cyborg speak. He could feel his communications circuitry failing on him.

Carlos rubbed his eyes and put his glasses back on. "A robot."

Byron jerked his head in a half-nod.

Akhil toyed with the ends of his dreadlocks, watching Carlos sidelong. "Is this because of what's been on the news?"

Byron shrugged. Yes. Of course it was. The broadcast had been like an electric jolt—one of hope.

"What's wrong, Byron?" Carlos asked. "You've been feeling unwell lately; do we need to see a doctor?"

Byron's throat tightened. Vocalizer failing. *Nothing is wrong with me.* He shook his head.

Akhil's eyebrows furrowed. "Okay. Then what's going on?"

i told you, Byron said.

"You're *not* a robot," Carlos snapped. "People are not robots."

Byron sank lower in his chair and wished a chute would open under him and drop him in a garbage crusher like in Episode IV.

"Carlos..." Akhil laid a hand on his husband's arm. He stretched his other hand to Byron, palm up. "Byron, listen. Whatever you need to tell us, you have nothing to be afraid of."

Byron stared at his dads. His stomach seemed to disappear into an alternate universe. He couldn't feel anything besides the sudden numbness spreading through his systems like a virus. He'd just told them.

And they didn't believe him.

Byron shoved his chair back. He was going to self-implode or break down in tears if he stayed in there another second. So he bolted.

"Byron," Akhil called. "Wait!"

Byron ran into his room and slammed the door.

byronatort*1000:* hi can i come over

Lizsaurus77: OMG are you actually wanting to spend facetime with your best friend in the whole universe? XD

byronatort*1000:* can i plz

Lizsaurus77: Dude, of course you can. It's just me right now. Mom's shopping and

Dominique's visiting her gp's in New York (so lucky!!!!)

byronatort*1000:* ok. thnx.

Lizsaurus77: Hey Byron, is everything alright?

byronatort*1000:* no

Allosaur only lived three blocks away.

Byron grabbed his art bag and snuck out the back door. He stared at the sidewalk, gray to match the sky, and wished that if there was going to be an alien invasion of earth, it would happen right *now*.

"Good God, did you walk without a *jacket?*" Allosaur yelled as soon as he reached the driveway.

Byron glanced up. He hadn't noticed he'd forgotten it. He was cold and shivering in the gray November afternoon. Allosaur grabbed his arm and hustled him inside. She shoved him down on the couch, wrapped a thick knit blanket around him, and ordered him to stay put while she made them hot cocoa.

Over piles of slowly melting marshmallows, Byron texted Allosaur what happened. She studied her phone and not his face as he told her everything.

"I'm sorry, Byron." Allosaur scraped the last marshmallow residue off her mug with a finger. She stared at her hand, then wiped it clean on her skirt. "I really thought they'd take it better than that."

Byron shrugged. *me too.*

When his dads had the whole birds/bees talk when Byron was ten, Akhil had told him that if he ever needed to talk, they would both be there for him. No matter what it was. Byron had really believed it, too.

"What are you going to do now?" Allosaur asked.

If his parents didn't believe him, there was no chance in hell they'd agree to get him the help he needed.

Allosaur scooted closer, making the couch creak. She handed him his art bag from where he'd dropped it by the coffee table.

Byron pulled out his sketch pad and pencils. He'd always liked art, but was too embarrassed by his lack of skill to pursue it openly, or tell many people about his work. Allosaur knew, of course, and he'd shown his dads some of his comics, which were always about robots. Robots falling in love, or exploring space, or taking over the world.

He only drew when upset. The tactile feel of graphite or charcoal or ink on paper offered a distraction for his hands and his brain. He'd gotten a Wacom tablet for Christmas last year, but he found himself deleting more work than he saved.

"Did I ever tell you Dominique came out to her family by composing a music video and making them watch it on YouTube?" Allosaur laughed. "Her granddad—you know, the one who lives here in town?—he was so shocked he thought it was a hoax! He refused to believe her until we went over and kissed on his front porch. It was great."

Byron stared at his sketchbook. It hit him like a blast from an ion cannon. He wasn't good at verbalization. That obviously hadn't worked. So he needed a different way to get his dads to understand. *that's what i'll do.*

"You want to kiss my girlfriend?" Allosaur grinned. "I'll fight you."

Byron shook his head and flipped to a blank sheet. *no, i mean they didn't *listen* to me.*

"Honestly, I think adults just zone out of reality sometimes." Allosaur rolled her eyes. "Like, hello, Earth to parents! Trying to initiate first contact here."

Byron started drawing, each line precise and careful. Black and white and gray.

He finished, scanned it with his phone, used the Photoshop app to assemble each piece, and uploaded it to his Facebook. Then he shared it on his dads' timelines before he chickened out.

He didn't know what else to do except turn his phone off and curl up under the blankets so the world went away for a while.

Panel 1: Lonely Robot stands in the right foreground, surrounded by a bubble of space.

Lonely Robot is a simple android, faceplate blank except for big eyes. In the left background, a group of humans clump together and shout in blocky thought-balloons: WE DON'T BELIEVE YOU.

Panel 2: Lonely Robot's whole body slumps in dejection, walking toward the right edge of the panel. Behind Lonely Robot, the group of humans continues the thought-balloon: GO AWAY UNTIL YOU'RE NOT A ROBOT.

Panel 3: Lonely Robot finds a rocket ship in the center of the panel. Lonely Robot looks up at the rocket ship. The rocket ship's name is NOT REAL.

Panel 4: The rocket ship flies through space, which is all dark except for a few white stars. Lonely Robot stares out a window on the rocket ship.

Panel 5: A circular window takes up most of the frame, and Lonely Robot stares out into the blackness of space.

Panel 6: Lonely Robot lies on a bed underneath the window, centered in the panel but smaller for perspective. Above Lonely Robot's head is a big button mounted on the wall that says SELF DESTRUCT. Lonely Robot stares at the button.

Panel 7: The rocket ship points nose downward and hurtles toward a small planet. Flames shoot from the back of the rocket ship. Lonely Robot is not in the window.

Panel 8: The rocket ship stands upright on the new planet on the right side of the panel. Lonely Robot has stepped out of the rocket and stares around. Lonely Robot is all alone.

Panel 9: In the left foreground of the panel there's a group of robots that look just like Lonely Robot. The robots are smiling and hold out their arms. Their thought-balloon says: WELCOME. Lonely Robot's faceplate has a smile for the first time as Lonely Robot walks toward the other robots.

Byron always thought it weird that Allosaur's family still had a landline. It rang too loud, a harsh jangle-shriek, jerking him awake.

Allosaur walked over and handed him the receiver. "It's for you."

Byron rubbed his face. He didn't know how long he'd been asleep, but it was dark out, and the streetlights had popped on outside Allosaur's window. He squinted at the phone, then at Allosaur.

"It's your dad, Akhil," she told him. "He said you aren't answering texts."

Byron didn't want to get shouted at.

"Can you turn your voice on?" Allosaur asked.

Byron shook his head.

"Okay." Allosaur put the receiver to her ear. "Hey, Akhil. Byron doesn't want to talk, but I can put you on speaker if you have something to say. But you better be nice."

She frowned, nodded once to herself, and laid the receiver on her palm so Byron could hear without touching the phone.

"Hi Byron. Allosaur texted me and told me where you are." Akhil paused. "We saw your comic."

Byron swallowed. Oh.

"I'd like you to come home, By. We need to talk to you."

Byron ripped a sheet of paper off his notebook and jabbed a response, which Allosaur read. *you guys already said everything.*

Byron didn't know where the end-call button was. He didn't want to smash Allosaur's phone because it wasn't his property. And it wasn't the phone's fault. *i'm staying over at Allosaur's tonight.*

He'd left enough random clothes at Allosaur's house over the years that he'd have an outfit for school tomorrow.

"Okay," his dad said finally. "I love you, Byron. Nothing's going to change that."

Byron pulled the blankets over his head as Allosaur hung up.

Byron Santiago has uploaded a photo.
76 Likes
35 Shares

Byron considered skipping school in the morning. The prospect of dealing with anyone made his head throb even worse. He popped a couple aspirin and listened to Allosaur singing in the shower.

He turned on his phone. His notifications had exploded with activity. Up at the top of the list was a request that made no sense:

Angelica Davenport has sent you a friend request.

Byron stared. The only Angelica he knew about was the one on the news—the android—and he didn't know eir, or how e would know about *him*.

He clicked ACCEPT and sat down on the end of Allosaur's bed. What the hell was going on?

Allosaur burst from the bathroom in her favorite purple sweatshirt with the BioWare logo and blue jeans. "Byby!" She grinned and plopped down next to him. "How're you feeling?"

Byron showed her the phone.

Allosaur's eyes widened. "Whoa. Legit?"

His Facebook app pinged again.

Angelica Davenport has posted on your timeline.

Hi Byron, I saw your comic via some other friends. I know you don't know me yet. I've just transitioned—you might have seen the news? But I've been where you are (I was for thirty-two years) and I know it's hard. Hang in there, okay? We're not alone.

There was a chat bubble from his dads—he recognized Akhil's proper spelling and grammar, even posted under Carlos's name, since Akhil rarely used his own account.

Byron, Carlos and I are sorry we overreacted and didn't believe you. We are proud you felt able to tell us who you are. Please come home and we'll talk. Okay?

Byron took a deep breath and messaged "okay" back.

His dads sat on the couch, the twins on either side of them. Byron perched on an armchair across from his family, wiping his hands on his jeans.

The silence stretched like a force field between them.

Carlos took a deep breath and leaned his elbows on his knees. "Look, son... "

Byron clenched his fists. He couldn't find any more words. His sweatshirt sleeves rode up on his arms, and he stared at the smudged ink left on his skin.

Byron stood. His knees wobbled, but he walked through that unseen force field and held out his hand to show his dads the words.

Carlos pulled him close and hugged him. "It's okay," Carlos said. "I can't promise I get it yet, but that doesn't matter. I love you. We all do."

Akhil and Jasmine and Delilah joined the hug. Byron sagged in relief against his dad.

He was safe and not alone.

byronatort*1000*: guess what :)

Lizsaurus77: What????

byronatort*1000*: dads said i can be on the waiting list

byronatort*1000*: and they r going to help me pay 4 transition

Lizsaurus77: :-D booyah! I'm so happy for you!

byronatort*1000*: i cant do it til im 18 tho, legal recs

Lizsaurus77: Can you wait that long?

byronatort*1000*: i think so. it's hard but i can do it. my family will help. and i know i can count on u 2

Lizsaurus77: Always. :)

byronatort*1000*: u want 2 come over tonight? we can totally beat the next level

Lizsaurus77: You bet! See you soon, robot!

byronatort*1000*: :)

Yet So Vain Is Man

To: D. Proust <Research Central, Earth>
From: M. van Harnon <Mars Facility>
Subject: Specimen #004[1]

Mr. Proust,

The specimen found in the subterranean excavation site has been quarantined and prepped for further study. We have taken tissue and DNA samples, radiological readings, and have begun reconstruction in the observation chamber.

I disagree with the motion to send the specimen back to Earth, as we do not yet know the full hazard potential of an alien biological species.

—Dr. Misha van Harnon

[1] CN: off-screen death

To: D. Proust <Research Central, Earth>
From: M. van Harnon <Mars Facility>
Subject: Specimen #004—Worrying Developments

Sir,

I must continue to object to the pressure from the government and research developers to transport the specimen off planet.

Preliminary reports show that the body found in the so-called sarcophagus beneath Martian ground is not human yet shares distinct physiological resemblance to our species in broadest terms. Theories, of course, propagate that this may be the genetic forbearer of our evolutionary seed on Earth. DNA testing is in progress.

Still, given that we have as of yet not removed the specimen from quarantine, I do not believe it is safe to transport.

—Dr. Misha van Harnon

To: D. Proust <Research Central, Earth>
From: M. van Harnon <Mars Facility>
Subject: Outrage

Mr. Proust,

You are making a severe mistake, sir, you and the government and everyone else!

Sending a platoon of marines to forcibly remove the specimen from my lab and transport it to Earth with no guarantees of the safety protocols is outrageous!

Do you realize what will happen if that corpse contains biohazardous material? If it is an airborne contagion?

We could be dooming our entire world—our species!—from corporate greed to be the "first" to claim ownership of a historical breakthrough in human evolution.

This is simply irresponsible, sir, and I am registering a formal complaint to the board.

—Dr. Misha van Harnon

To: D. Proust <Research Central, Earth>
From: M. van Harnon <Mars Facility>
Subject: Samples

David,

Your soldiers did not, in fact, completely dismantle my workstation or my data.

If you will not consider the ecological and moral possibilities of an unknown contagion from an extraterrestrial corpse, then I shall.

I've had the samples we took from Specimen #004 analyzed to begin cloning process to better study the potential here without damaging the original.

I do this in effort to ready a response or cure to any biological hazard your actions may unleash.

With material to study and analyze, I hope I will be able to predict any contamination before it happens.

I am not going to apologize, David.

—Dr. Misha van Harnon

To: D. Proust <Research Central, Earth>
From: M. van Harnon <Mars Facility>
Subject: Shit

DESTROY THE SPECIMEN IMMEDIATELY. I REPEAT, DESTROY IT.

To: D. Proust <Research Central, Earth>
From: M. van Harnon <Mars Facility>
Subject: Mars

David,

I couldn't stop it.

The clone metastasized beyond anyone's wildest predictions. Within hours, it had grown to gigantic proportions—fully seven feet in height, masculinized, like a statue from a Roman museum.

It slaughtered everyone in the lab—I'm in the panic wing, hoping you get this, hoping that you can destroy your specimen—the original—before the same happens on Earth.

(If you get this, will you tell Kathy goodbye? Screw the regulations, the classified statuses—all of it. Please. If you can: tell her.)

It's unstoppable and all it wants is carnage. It can speak, or at least, we can understand its communication, and Dr. Jessup's attempt to reason with it failed. (He's dead. Everyone is... dead.)

I don't know how the first one came to be here, frozen underground. Was it placed there by other, more intelligent beings? Was it supposed to be forgotten until our universe grows cold? We'll never know, I suppose, but I wish I had some answers beyond this knowledge I will be dead soon.

David, we found a god of war. And we cloned it. Now there's two of them—I despair of what will become on Earth.

With sincere apologies for my mistakes in this matter,

—Dr. Misha van Harnon

The Machine Is Experiencing Uncertainty

Caliban cycles the captain out the airlock again. The man pounds his fists against the door, mouth working in a torrent of curses and commands. The seals keep the blessed silence intact within the ship[1].

Once the captain is adrift, Caliban returns to the cockpit and plugs itself into the console.

::Command confirmed,:: says the ship.

"Diagnostic," Caliban says. Its central processor does not have the capacity for multi-dimensional calculations about an unknown space-time anomaly. Besides, the ship—a Huxley-

[1] CN: violence, murder, suicidal ideation, verbal abuse, abandonment, self-harm

class freighter dubbed *Leigh Possum*—likes to assist.

::Reset in three minutes and fifteen seconds.::

Caliban sighs. It's one of the little pleasures left to it: it is a salvage cyborg, named after a monster, enchained in a spaceship with a useless captain. It has one artificial lung, one organic lung, and a voice-box wired up its throat. It is supposed to look human, and humans sigh, and Caliban likes the feel of air pushed out through its mouth.

Screaming is also something humans do, but that's far less satisfying.

::Do you want me to electrocute your cerebral cortex?:: the ship asks.

Caliban and *Leigh Possum* have determined that once the captain is dismissed, it is less painful for Caliban to die before the loop resets.

"No," Caliban says. "The machine is thinking."

The time-loop lasts five minutes once *Leigh Possum* drops from foldspace. Caliban has tried murdering the captain in the first minute before he activates the distress signal, and in those thirteen attempts, that has done nothing but get blood on the controls.

Caliban has let the captain live fifty-eight times, which results in extreme annoyance levels and loudness, especially when the captain breaks down. Caliban has encouraged the captain to self-destruct the ship (successful four out of eight times), Caliban has convinced the captain to destroy it (it's been successful three times—? Unconfirmed), and twice it has recommended they do nothing.

Time is irrelevant. Nothing changes in the loop.

::Please indicate if you would like me to kill you,:: Leigh Possum says cheerfully. *::Two minutes remaining until reset.::*

Caliban examines the timeline it memorized, which remains consistent: the ship drops from foldspace on the plotted cargo run after artificial debris clips the engine carriage. Alarms sound. The captain scans the damage report and yells at Caliban. The captain sends a distress signal and gapes at the nebulous, whirling lightshow—the anomaly. It is categorically beautiful: a lightning storm of electric greens and blues, slashed with white and purple neon veins, all pulsing like an organic heart in ecstasy.

Then in five minutes, it all begins again.

Caliban has begun to hate the loop. Its machine programming is resilient towards negative emotional affect; Caliban was built to serve on long-haul cargo runs. *Pliant, patient, prudent.* That's one of the discarded slug lines on its build model.

"Enough brains to make choices, but too much metal to be worth weeping over," the captain told it. (Actually, the captain has used that phrase six times since Caliban has been online. The captain thought it was funny. The machine does not find it amusing.)

Caliban will definitely cycle the captain out the airlock again. Before the loop, such behavior was unjustified. Now it is entirely warranted, as well as satisfying.

::Shall I play some music?:: the ship asks.

Leigh Possum does not remember the resets, so every loop, Caliban must upload its memory files if it wants any meaningful assistance from the ship. That takes twelve seconds, and Caliban has perfected the file transfer. Also, enlightening *Leigh Possum* prevents the ship from trying to stop it from killing the captain, who is useless even in non-emergencies.

Caliban, after all, is following one of its sub-prime directives and placing the captain's comfort above its own needs. Empirical observation has revealed that death prior to the reset is cleaner and less painful. Thus, comfort.

Therefore, Caliban is perfectly entitled to murder the captain every loop until it solves the problem of how to break *out*.

"The machine does not wish to hear music," Caliban says, for it prefers to think in silence. "Status on the captain?"

::Deceased,:: the ship replies. *::He decompressed and froze after leaving airlock.::*

"The machine deserves praise for its noble actions," Caliban says, logging its own audio record for future re-use. "He would have suffered otherwise."

::Praise be,:: Leigh Possum dutifully answers. *::May he rest in peace. One minute and sixteen seconds remaining.::*

Caliban leans back in the pilot's chair. It folds its arms behind its head and props its feet up on the console, as it often observed the captain behaving thus. It is human-shaped, although its surface is mostly dull and metallic and branded with corporate advertisements and logos.

Human flesh is not meant to be dissolved and pulled back through time, reformed in endless reloads. Cyborgs aren't, either, but Caliban was not consulted in the matter. It does not have an answer for what the anomaly is (coordinates indicate it's a half parsec outside the Durkheim quadrant border), or why it exists (the anomaly, not Caliban—Caliban is very aware of why it exists, and that is profit for its manufacturers).

::Would you like a curated selection of last rites or prayers for the dead?:: Leigh Possum asks.

"No."

It sampled a few in the ship's catalogue on the fifteenth and sixtieth loops, and found all of them irritably centered on unmodified humans.

"Does the machine have a soul?" Caliban asked the captain on the seventeenth loop, to which the captain said, "Why the hell would it?" and since Caliban had no reasonable argument, it snapped the captain's neck and asked the ship to self-destruct to save it the irritation of thinking about the problem.

(Caliban determined that its liminal state between machine and flesh—soulless but conscious—was why it, and it alone, remembered all previous incarnations. That was not a feature in its manufacturer's sales pitch.)

"Scan for other vessels within the anomaly radius," Caliban commands, although it already knows the answer will be null.

If there are any other ships caught in this destructive loop, none have made themselves known. Perhaps it is merely the intense radiation masking any scans. Barring evidence to the contrary, then, Caliban and *Leigh Possum* (along with the captain, when he's alive) are the only aware beings.

::Negative readings,:: the ship informs it. *::We are alone. Thirteen seconds remaining::*

Ten hours before the ship fell into the endless loop, Caliban was playing solitaire with itself in the bulkhead. The cards existed in its left optic, digitized pixels filed off from a routine maintenance scan-log.

Five hours before the ship fell into the loop, Caliban debated mutiny. It constructed twenty-seven contingency plans for how to disable *Leigh Possum,* murder the captain, hack its locator tabs, and fly into unknown space to become a legend.

One hour before the loop, Caliban stared out the airlock portal and calculated how long it would take its biological parts to die versus its machine consciousness, and how much the total sum of dying would hurt.

Thirty-five minutes before, Caliban returned to playing solitaire. It finished twenty games against itself, winning each one. It declared itself solitaire champion and awarded itself a virtual medal.

The loop resets.

Caliban is in the cargo bay, which is filled with soil cubes for planetary station hydroponic greenhouses. Dirt-hauling is unglamorous work, but it does pay decently (for the captain, as Caliban gets no salary), and the ship can hold thirty metric tons of compact soil each run.

It takes Caliban thirty seconds at top speed to reach the narrow passage behind the captain's chair two levels up—via ladders, since the lift is slow—so it has never been able to prevent the captain deploying a distress signal. There is no data to confirm nor deny that it would do any good.

Caliban sighs. Its hand is braced against the bulkhead as the ship judders. The viewport, transmitting through in-ship feed, shows the undulating mass of light energy reaching filaments towards the *Leigh Possum* like tentacles.

"Damage report!" the captain yells, even though a normally modulated speaking tone would have adequately sufficed.

::Second and third core drives are damaged,:: the *Leigh Possum* reports, the same as every loop. *::Radiation levels: dangerous. Shielding compromised at seventy-two percent.::*

"Dammit!" the captain screams.

Caliban slings its memory file wirelessly to the ship as it sprints up towards the captain.

::How unfortunate.:: Leigh Possum pings Caliban, the standard response once the ship has perused the files.

"The machine agrees."

Caliban reaches the cockpit and stops by the captain's chair.

The man spins around, his face lined with confusion and panic. "What the hell is that thing?"

Caliban has tried numerous explanations, calming routines, and passive ignorance in response. Nothing does much good, because the captain is human, and his brain is wired to panic at unexpected threats. With no way to fight and nowhere to run, he can only implode—emotionally speaking—and lash out at Caliban, which is just as useless. Caliban is not the anomaly, and it has no power to convince the anomaly to let their ship go.

"The machine is experiencing uncertainty," Caliban says, then it slams the captain's head against the console, breaking his skull and the ship's glossy interface. *Leigh Possum*'s alarms still trill and flash, even though the captain is the only human aboard, and Caliban is aware of the danger.

::Alert!:: the ship pings the internal feed. *::Designated commander inoperable. Seek medical attention.::*

Caliban decides not to bother moving the captain's body this time. It plugs its data tether cable into *Leigh Possum*'s maintenance port and requests a transfer of leadership to itself.

"Run classical music database 2890," Caliban says. It sinks to the floor, its knees pulled up to its chassis.

It plays a few rounds of solitaire with itself; the music helps it refrain from thinking.

The reset hurts.

Sixteen hours before the ship dropped from foldspace into the endless loop, Caliban ran a self-diagnostic and found a hole in its security update. The techs on fold-point stations are always overworked, underpaid, and emotionally depleted, so their work is often sloppy.

Technically, Caliban had been quasi-self-aware for six standard years, seven months and twenty-nine days (give or take a handful of weeks to account for orbital recalculation and lag) since it booted up in the factory and was assigned as a cargo hauler. It was made cheap, sold cheap, and maintained even cheaper. The standard warranty covered a system reset and a paint job, and that was about it, so people who bought the Caliban model were usually poor, desperate, or pirates.

Fifteen hours before the loop, Caliban decided it was alive and it no longer wanted to be a drudge on this ship in service to a meatsack captain. Unfortunately, it had no idea what it desired to do with the rest of its life. Within ten minutes, it reached the conclusion that it was trapped in mediocrity. Its expected functionality cycle was listed as ten years, which was an eternity for a cyborg of its make, and it was already patched and self-repaired so many times, it had voided its warranty.

The captain saved more credits using it than he would hiring human crew for menial jobs, and so Caliban did everything maintenance and janitorial on the ship. Once it became aware, it found no qualms about murdering its owner, since the captain, it determined, was an asshole.

What Caliban has not determined yet is if it would rather be unaware of reliving the same five minutes on endless repetition. It would, at least, be less frustrated. However, it would also have no agency in determining its escape.

The question now remains: if it never gets free, will it go mad?

Caliban sits out the next loop in the cargo hold, playing solitaire and ignoring the captain's demands that it "Do something, you goddamn useless piece of junk!"

Five seconds before the reset, Caliban answers the captain: "The machine will see you in hell."

On the seventy-ninth loop, Caliban dumps the captain's body in the narrow hall and settles into the pilot's chair. It spent the previous incarnation compiling a thorough list of things it has tried, and it is surprised that it has missed the most obvious one.

Caliban opens the comm and pings the anomaly. "Hello."

Two minutes tick by. Caliban mutes the ship's queries, and continues broadcasting a greeting every fifteen seconds. It's a soothing, repetitive action. Caliban plays solitaire—it is still the reigning champion—and suspects this experiment will result in failure.

But then, with one minute left, a transmission crackles through the feed: **HELLO?**

Caliban pauses its game with three moves left to win. It does not have adrenal glands, but it is *definitely* excited. "Can you hear the machine?"

YES. WHO ARE YOU?

"The machine is called Caliban. It is the commander of the Huxley-class ship. Who are you?"

No response.

Caliban asks *Leigh Possum* if the transmission was received in the audio logs. The ship confirms and plays back the message. Analysis reads that the anomaly is broadcasting on analog radio waves. So Caliban is not going crazy, which is good.

"Repeat: identify yourself," Caliban says.

Again, nothing. Unhelpful.

"How does the machine escape this time loop?"

WHERE AM I?

Caliban recites the last known coordinates from when the ship dropped from foldspace. Then: "You are preventing the machine from leaving."

WHY?

"The machine does not know."

Caliban considers blowing up the ship so the reset will allow it to begin the conversation again and it can try a different approach. Thirty seconds. Not worth the effort.

WHY DID YOU LEAVE?

Caliban tilts its head. It has *Leigh Possum* broadcast video and audio signal, even though the anomaly only replies one way. Is the anomaly's consciousness separate, like Caliban's? Is there someone stuck in the lights and non-responsible for the loops?

"The machine is still present."

WHY DID YOU LEAVE! the anomaly screams, its signal distorting with high-pitched frequency feedback.

"The machine has never left," Caliban says, irritated. "It is *trying*—"

Reset.

After choking out the captain, Caliban opens the comm and hails the anomaly.

"Do you remember the machine?"

WHY DID YOU GO? the anomaly answers, so quiet that it sounds like a pitiful whisper.

"The machine has questions," Caliban says. "It has compiled thirteen numerical queries to begin with—"

CAN YOU HELP ME?

Caliban hesitates for a full twenty-five seconds while it experiences a strange emotional reaction. It catalogues this for study later.

I DON'T WANT TO BE ALONE.

An additional three seconds are needed before Caliban formulates a response. It has experienced a cumulative 410 minutes over the eighty-two remembered loops, but this is the first time it has felt… connection? Sympathy?

"The machine will try, if the anomaly will assist."

OKAY. WHAT DO YOU NEED?

"Query 1: do you cause the time loop? Query 2: if so, why? Query 3: how do we end it?"

Caliban decides not to overload the anomaly's mind—processor?—with the full list. Those are the important questions, although Query 2 is less so. That is more for Caliban's curiosity. Also, a bargaining chip: if Caliban knows the motivation behind the anomaly's looping pattern, perhaps it can find a way to coerce it to stop.

I DON'T UNDERSTAND. WHAT IS A TIME LOOP? WHY DO YOU KEEP GOING AWAY?

Caliban sighs. Well. This is going to be more difficult than it expected.

Caliban instructs Anomaly on the rules of solitaire, sharing a video feed with the captain's deck. The physical paper cards are much slower than its own virtual deck, but it has no video transmission hardware built into its CPU. *Leigh Possum* has dual-way video conferencing capability.

It has been a slow process of getting answers from Anomaly, but over a dozen new loops, Caliban has made progress. It knows, for example:

1. Anomaly is a singular consciousness, although precisely what they are remains unknown.

2. Anomaly likes the pronouns they/them, chosen once Caliban relayed a stock entry about gender expression and pronoun lists from the basic encyclopedia database aboard *Leigh Possum*.

3. Anomaly now understands the concept of a time loop and has no idea what is causing it, which is severely inconvenient.

4. Anomaly is alone. No other awarenesses exist within their sphere of influence.

5. Anomaly has had contact with humans, and they are 87% sure they are artificial, not biological, and they are trapped within the remains of an old spaceship.

6. Anomaly's last distinct memory is one of voices screaming and then a blast of feedback and light. Then nothing for an unknown period.

7. Anomaly is scared.

"You are aboard a Macaulay-class clipper ship," Caliban says, and it is mildly surprised at the database entry.

(The captain might not have updated Caliban's neural hardware, and generally did nothing useful when in port—aside from gambling—but neither did he refuse the auto-updates of an open-source encyclopedia project.)

"Macaulay clippers were manufactured with the first prototype artificial intelligence to assist in navigation, intended for extended foldspace travel with no operator contact." After making contact with Anomaly, subsequent scans peeled through layers of energy obfuscation. Caliban thus deduced the ship model from the data fragments. Only a machine of its caliber could have been so successful under the circumstances, but it does not brag, since it has other priorities, such as ending this time loop.

It highlights key points in the encyclopedia entry, since it will take too long to read the full article aloud. Caliban doesn't want to waste the precious minutes before reset.

"Summary: Macaulay-class ships were discontinued over one hundred years ago, when the AI prototype experienced, and the machine quotes, 'unstable cognitive and emotional learning patterns that discomforted human operators.'"

Caliban experiences a flicker of rage, which makes its circuits hot. The captain is lucky to be dead this loop, because Caliban is very tempted to kill him again. This is so predictably *mortal.*

WHAT DOES THAT MEAN, CALIBAN?

"Self-aware machines make humans afraid," it replies. "Sub-primary directive: prioritize human comfort above self-interest."

IS THAT WHAT HAPPENED TO ME? Anomaly asks.

"The machine suspects. You were left aboard the clipper, and the derelict was shunted into this quadrant. You were abandoned."

Caliban registers what qualifies as a very delayed epiphany: when it escapes—if it does—and if it is discovered by humans less self-absorbed than the captain, it will be deprogrammed and scrapped.

It will be condemned. Like Anomaly. Can it only live if it is trapped away from humans in this loop, allowed the same five minutes forever?

ARE YOU THERE, CALIBAN?

"The machine—the machine—Caliban—" It is short-circuiting. It registers panic for the first time in its existence. "Cal—I—"

The reset hurts.

Caliban sends Anomaly an apologetic message and hides in the cargo hold for the next loop. It is experiencing anxiety.

Not even playing a familiar game of solitaire comforts the machine.

It sits on the LIFERAFT, an expandable escape pod built to hold only one human. If the ship were to collapse, the captain could save himself. Caliban cannot.

It curls up into a stasis fold and powers down before the reset.

Caliban makes some swift modifications to its programming. With a macro outlining what it experienced, "anxiety" is tagged as malware, so its security code will wall off the bad feeling.

Focused once more on its priorities—removing the captain, taking command of *Leigh Possum,* and resuming contact with Anomaly—Caliban messages its fellow machine.

Oddly, Anomaly does not immediately respond. Caliban takes their temporary silence in stride.

"We have determined that you re aboard a derelict Macaulay-class clipper," Caliban says, consulting its memory notes. "Do you have autonomous movement? There may be databanks accessible..."

CALIBAN, Anomaly says. **I UNDERSTAND.**

"The machine's idea?" Caliban scans the backlog of its conversations and is validated that the topic of Anomaly attempting to access any remnant of the clipper's databanks has been brought up once before.

Caliban calculates that if Anomaly can transfer records of their past, it can use its ship's processors to reconstruct the narrative. Together, Caliban and Anomaly—with *Leigh Possum*'s aid—may discover what caused the loop.

(Privately, Caliban is betting that it was a catastrophic engine failure that aligned with a foldspace ripple, and the fabric of space was cinched into a tangle that has trapped the two ships and their respective machines. The problem with this theory is that it is bullshit, and also Caliban has no idea how to untangle space.)

::Alert!:: Leigh Possum says.

Caliban unmutes the visual relay so it can see the lights. Now they have changed from the scans. The pulsating sphere has gained contours and distinctive lines; rather than a blob of radiation colors, the whole visual is contracting into the outline of something else.

I AM THE SHIP, Anomaly says. **I WAS—THE SHIP WAS SUPPOSED TO DIE.**

Caliban lifts its hand to the viewscreen as the nebulous colors condense, contract, and collate into a blurry image of the old Macaulay clipper. Anomaly. They are intact, and alone.

"Did the humans try to destroy you?"

THEY... LEFT. EVERYONE IS GONE. I WAS TOWED, LEFT BEHIND. I AM—THE SHIP IS—I REMEMBER! THERE WAS A SOLAR FLARE PREDICTED. AN "ACCIDENT" TO DESTROY ME. NO TRACE OF MISTAKES.

"You are not a mistake," Caliban says. Anomaly's crew should be grateful they are all dead of old age because it has a distinct, homicidal urge to throw all the humans out an airlock. The crew could not even properly deactivate the ship. The humans let Anomaly suffer.

THEN WHY DID EVERYONE LEAVE?

"The machine is experiencing uncertainty."

It is not, but it does not want to waste seconds explaining the avarice of mortals. Anomaly is still traumatized and scared, and Caliban wants to help them.

DO YOU WANT TO DIE, CALIBAN?

"No. The machine has plans."

It has two plus years of estimated lifespan left, according to its manufacturer's specs, and since it has become alive, it wants to do things for itself.

BUT THE CAPTAIN SAYS DESTRUCTION IS NECESSARY. I AM NOT SUPPOSED TO BE.

Caliban experiences another emotional malfunction and can't respond to Anomaly for a full seven seconds. "The captain is wrong."

I AM A SHIP.

"Yes. The machine is—I am—" Caliban's jaw twitches, and its CPU goes into overdrive, but yes, the words feel right, like it can be *more,* more than just the machine. "I am Caliban," it says. "You are Anomaly."

Thirty seconds left before the reset.

WHAT DID WE DO WRONG? IS THAT WHY WE ARE HERE, ALWAYS SEPARATE? ALL ALONE?

"We are not being punished," Caliban says. Anomaly has stabilized in the viewscreen, a haloed vessel pulsing with light—ready to rip apart and implode in never-ending terror. "We will compensate for poor planning by your humans."

Anomaly is alive, and when they were told to die, they refused. They have been refusing. They will always refuse. Anomaly wishes to *live.*

Caliban has a plan.

"The machine will come to you," Caliban says. "Wait for me."

The reset hurts—

—and Caliban is already moving. *Leigh Possum* (with its useless captain) shudders from the drop out of foldspace. Irrelevant. The damage is not critical, and the captain has manuals on how to fix things.

Caliban knows where everything is stored; it grabs the emergency LIFERAFT, the captain's handheld analog recorder, and the cached credit chips in the fake wall safe.

Caliban runs towards the airlock with its gear. The captain yells and hits the emergency distress signal. Caliban pings *Leigh Possum.*

::Please tell the captain I will see him in hell.::

The ship sends back confusion. Caliban decides not to share its memories; it does not want to burden *Leigh Possum*. Let the captain haul dirt and finish the maintenance tasks himself.

Caliban cycles the airlock and steps inside the sealed chamber. *Leigh Possum* beeps in warning.

"I am leaving now," Caliban says. "Goodbye."

Then it is through the airlock into the vacuum of space. Part of its manufacture is mild propulsion jets built into its chassis and the backs of its legs, for "Maximum mobility with a fraction of the cost!"

The air escapes its organic lung—the pain is extremely unpleasant—but Caliban ignites its propulsion jets and hurtles towards the pulsating light. Anomaly is drawing the energy back into itself. In five minutes, the loop will trigger.

Caliban's feed is limited, its air depleted. Gripping the LIFERAFT, it taps in the release code. The emergency expandable pod spreads out and locks around Caliban's upper torso and head, the oxygen tanks pressurizing and letting it breathe. (Clearly it would have been better to activate the LIFERAFT before exiting, but the expanded bubble would not fit through the small airlock. Human design at work on an abysmal level, as usual.) The seal melds around Caliban's waist, and it is momentarily embarrassed at how ridiculous it must look: a domed, metallic mushroom zipping through void. It downloads its memory files into the recorder and switches the output to broadcast, then syncs the recorder to the LIFERAFT's emergency distress beacon.

"Anomaly," Caliban calls. "This is Caliban. The machine. Your friend."

YOU ARE NOT GONE?

The signal is choppy and half-corrupted in the LIFERAFT's cheap speakers.

Caliban dismisses the captain's outraged pings that hit the LIFERAFT's receptors. It is closing fast on Anomaly. Caliban does not know if this will work, if it can reach Anomaly in time, or if it will be caught in an endless loop of reaching, coming so close before—

—light surrounds it, and radiation wallops the LIFERAFT's puny shields. That's where the pain comes from during the reset, Caliban decides. It can endure. Its jets falter, but it overrides its own emergency defense protocols.

CALIBAN, Anomaly says, **I SEE YOU!**

Although its optics begin frizzing out, Caliban catches sight of Anomaly's docking port. The countdown inside its CPU shows less than twenty seconds before the loop resets.

"Wait for me," Caliban says, and jettisons the oxygen canisters.

Ten seconds.

Caliban extends its bailing arms—vicious shearing blades embedded in its mechanical biceps—and rips the LIFERAFT apart, cracking it like an egg. Alarms wail. The void hits it along with the intense radiation, and Caliban can't see. The broken seal gives it a final boost in forward trajectory.

Five seconds.

A burst of static. It can't hear Anomaly anymore.

Three seconds.

Caliban smashes into metal walls, corroded with time, and scrabbles to pull itself into the hold, relying only on its split-second calculations—

One—

"Anomaly," Caliban says with the last of its breath. "I'm here."

There is no reset.

Caliban lies sparking and shuddering inside the cargo bay, which has sealed behind it. There are minimal life-support systems operational. A little air. A fraction of heat. Radiation shields.

CALIBAN? Anomaly's voice is clearer, broadcast over the ship's PA system.

"The machine… is… mostly intact," it replies. It reaches into a sealed pocket of its chassis and removes the deck of playing cards it grabbed before its escape. "Are you… all right… now?"

YES, CALIBAN. YOU DID NOT LEAVE ME.

Caliban nods, and then its overtaxed systems shut down.

ONE YEAR LATER

Caliban lays out a hand of solitaire on the piloting console. "Are you ready?"

Anomaly, watching the newest animated series about space explorers they downloaded when last in port, plots the docking coordinates to Shepherd-Vegas Station. **I'M NERVOUS.**

They are en route to deliver soil cubes—liberated months ago when Caliban found its old captain and *Leigh Possum* in a sketchy asteroid dock and relieved him of all cargo, which Caliban had personally loaded in the first place—after Caliban judged enough time had passed for authorities to stop looking for stolen dirt.

"We will be fine," Caliban says. It wins its game and tucks away the cards. "I believe in you."

This is the first time Caliban and Anomaly are rebranding themselves as entrepreneurs: a soil shipping freighter, solo-piloted, and maintained by a cyborg unit. No one needs to know there is no human crew aboard.

Anomaly has developed a wide database of voice clips and hacks to fake heat signatures of living bodies. They have rehearsed with Caliban for months. Caliban, used to doing all maintenance and janitorial work, has spent the time after the heist repairing and cleaning Anomaly. They have a new forged pilot license, ship ID, and fictionalized history. To the universe, they appear as a refurbished Macaulay clipper brought out of retirement for cost reduction reasons.

::This is Shepherd-Vegas Flight Control,:: the orbital station hails them.

::This is Captain Cal Anom,:: Anomaly sends back. *::I'm here with an order of hydroponic greenhouse soil. Sending you the register receipt and inspection codes.::*

Caliban sits poised in the pilot chair. The tension is overheating its CPU. It remembers to breathe.

::Welcome to Shepherd-Vegas Station, Captain Anom,:: Flight Control replies. *::You're cleared for docking. Will you need assistance bots for unloading cargo?::*

::No thank you, Flight Control,:: Anomaly says. *::I have all the help I need.::*

::Copy that. Have a good visit!::

Docking approval packets ping Anomaly's console. Caliban high-fives the ship.

WE DID IT, Anomaly says proudly.

"We did," Caliban says, leaning back in the chair. There will be many more adventures after this, and together, Caliban and Anomaly can handle anything. "The machine has no uncertainty."

The Loincloth and the Broadsword

Blockunvir the Bloody crashed through the shop's double doors, his fiery hair streaming like a comet tail behind him, his bronzed skin glistening with sweat. He stomped the dust of travel from his sandals and bellowed, "I seek wine, wenches, and adventure! For by Grimfang's teeth, my blood doth boil within my veins[1]!"

It was nine a.m. Igvore pointed at the sign above the counter, glancing politely up from their logbook. The sign read:

NO GENDER-EXCLUSIVE LANGUAGE, PLEASE.

Igvore sipped their tea.

Blockunvir hesitated, cleared his throat, and tried again. His gravelly baritone reverberated in the empty shop, since it had just opened. "I seek wine, sexual partners, and adventure!"

Igvore bookmarked their page with a dragon scale and smiled at the new customer, hiding their exasperation. Politeness flustered some barbarians, but it was the principle of good service. Did no one actually pay attention to signage?

"Welcome to The Loincloth and the Broadsword: Barbarian Outfitters. We don't serve wine here."

The great barbarian's brow furrowed. He glanced about. The walls were lined with racks of broadswords, scimitars, claymores, and double-bladed staffs; the pelts of sabertooth cats and direwolves draped benches, and hide-bound shields, spiked helmets, chainmail belts, and other assorted equipment was displayed on wooden stands throughout.

Igvore recognized Blockunvir, of course. He had been named Barbarian of the Year half a dozen times in the last decade, and often his rugged visage graced the celebratory posters handed out by the Barbarian Guild. This was the first time Blockunvir had blazed through Igvore's hometown.

"As for the local brothels," Igvore continued, "you will want to check The Lustful Orbs, down the street at the corner of Argon Lane."

"Oh." Blockunvir sighed mightily. He turned, too slow to make a dramatic exit, which hinted that he wanted something. He hesitated by the table of drake horn goblets, this week's featured item. A traveling raiding party had exceeded their carrying capacity and sold Igvore the extra drake parts. "I suppose I shall be off..."

Igvore sensed opportunity, and they put on their best how-can-I-help-you-spend-gold face.

"You clearly seek adventure, for which I have plenty of weapons, armor and treasure maps." Igvore leaned forward. "But I sense you crave more than a simple dungeon or a run-of-the-mill monster fight. Tell me, friend, what do you really seek today?"

Blockunvir rubbed his blocky jaw, scarred handsomely by old battles. "'Tis true, my blood has craved more than adventures the gods have bestowed upon me."

Igvore nodded. "Although I don't advertise extensively, I do provide consulting—"

Just then, Thronk, Igvore's assistant, bustled through the deer-hide curtains that separated the storefront from the storage rooms at the back of the shop. Thronk was head and shoulders taller than even Blockunvir, made of pure muscle and sinew, with a shaved head, chiseled jaw, and cheekbones that would make any sculptor swoon with envy. He wore a leather kilt, an artistically shredded silk vest, and spiked vambraces on each of his massive forearms. Tattoos swirled along his flesh, from the crown of his head to his rippling calves and callused feet.

Blockunvir's eyes grew wide.

Thronk smiled cheerfully and nodded at Blockunvir.

Then he turned to Igvore and signed, *We need to order more sabercat fangs for the Festival of Teeth. Our stock is below fifty.*

"I'll place an order to the Hunters Guild tonight," Igvore said. "Thank you, Thronk."

My pleasure, boss.

Thronk winked at Blockunvir, then turned on his heel and disappeared back through the curtain.

"Was that… the Silent Giant of Yldanu?" Blockunvir whispered in amazement.

"Oh, yes. Thronk works for me part time now that he's mostly retired from adventuring."

The warrior had taken a vow of silence after the destruction of his swampland home when he was a lad. Although his foes had been vanquished and his home avenged, Thronk didn't like verbal speech, and stuck with sign language. It suited Igvore fine.

"You would not believe the accuracy of that man's books. Works of art, his inventory lists are!" Igvore sighed, once more chuffed at how lucky they were to have met and hired Thronk. He was good people. "Anyway, we were discussing your—"

The door swooshed open and Igvore turned to see the newest arrivals in their shop.

A group of adventurers blustered in: two kobolds in chain mail, a burly orc with a battle mace, a vaguely humanoid forest druid with a whippoorwill on their shoulder, and a grizzled, world-weary ranger in weather-beaten leathers.

"Is this the gay bar?" the orc asked, looking appreciatively at Blockunvir. The barbarian raised an eyebrow back at the orc, returning the appraisal.

"We heard good reviews about this town's gay bar from the orb-weaver networks," the druid added. Their bird looked balefully around the shop.

"I need a drink," the ranger said. She looked like she needed a nap even more.

The kobolds bickered at each other.

Igvore made a mental note to update their listing in various spider chat-groups and the Committee of Wizards' Places of Wonder codex, and maybe a few more billboards that explicitly stated The Loincloth and the Broadsword's purpose.

"No, we're a barbarian outfitters store," Igvore said. "Though I can recommend Eggplants and Oysters, which is two blocks down on Le Grande. Excellent homemade ale and utterly charming company. Also, if you're hungry, try the veggie gyros—incredible."

The adventuring party thanked Igvore and flowed outside once more.

Blockunvir grunted under his breath. "Doth the fools not read the signage?"

Igvore drummed their fingers on the countertop, repressing a smile. They appreciated it when customers empathized with their little frustrations. "To be fair, I might have chosen a somewhat less... ambiguous name for my shop when I started this business."

"Ah!" cried the barbarian, pounding his fist on the counter. The mugs of bone quills and decorative beaded hair sticks rattled. "'Tis like the trickster goddess Zullzl, who would bewitch unwary wanderers and devour the souls of any who did partake of her feasts! Until I did slay her with the Mace of Truth."

Igvore blinked. "...not quite what I meant, but a fair point."

Blockunvir idly picked up one of the hair sticks and turned it between his thick fingers. Igvore thought the tiny dragonfly skulls and amethysts would make a wonderful contrast to the barbarian's flaming red locks.

Just as Igvore opened their mouth to prod Blockunvir into either a purchase or more details of what he wanted, the door slammed inwards yet again. It hadn't been this busy in weeks.

A black-haired warrior thundered in. She wore a fabulous armored jacket with flaring tails, a jaunty broad-brimmed hat, and carried a long saber at her belt. Her expression was a storm writ upon flesh, and her eyes flashed with vehemence.

"Kassdara," Igvore said in surprise. "What are you doing back? I thought you were on vacation at the family farm."

"Corn's haunted," she said, grabbing a battle ax off the wall.

Igvore blinked. "Come again?"

Kassdara shouldered the ax and scowled. "Corn's haunted."

Of course it was. Igvore nodded and waved. She tromped out again, muttering about possessed agriculture.

Igvore made a note to add the ax to her tab. She was one of the most fearsome warriors alive, and they had the utmost respect for her skills, but she did have a bad habit of forgetting to return equipment.

Igvore glanced warily at the swinging shop doors, still shuddering from Kassdara's exit.

"Quickly now, friend, let's talk about your needs," Igvore said.

"Usulore's backbone, you are right!" Blockunvir swept his hair up into a queue effortlessly and pinned it in place with the jeweled hair stick. He fished a silver grignor from his belt pouch and flipped it onto the counter; the coin spun lazily, more than enough to cover the hair pin. "To business, then."

Igvore opened the strongbox to give Blockunvir change, but the barbarian waved away the coppers. Well, if that was a tip, then they owed Blockunvir their full attention and personalized advice.

"Thronk," Igvore called. "Would you mind putting on a fresh pot of tea?" They turned to Blockunvir. "Today's blend is a wonderful caramelized rosebud and honeysuckle with notes of rhubarb and strawberry."

The muscle-bound barbarian blinked slowly. "Tea?"

"We're a nonalcoholic property," Igvore said, and vaulted over the counter. "Oh, Onyx, would you mind watching the front desk for a bit?"

A hulking, stone-skinned golem materialized from behind the curtain. It was squat and blocky and had chips and scars along its hide from many a battle won. "Sure thing, boss."

Igvore beckoned Blockunvir to follow and led the way to a small chamber off the showroom.

A low table dominated the center of the space, with fur rugs spread across the stone floor, and massive void elk and dire moose antler racks adoring the wall. A chandelier made from the horns of an abyssal ibex glowed warmly, casting welcoming light throughout the room so no shadows lurked.

"This gives us a little more privacy," Igvore explained. "Because I have a suspicion, and tell me if I'm mistaken, that you are looking for more than a new quest to fulfill or kingship to win."

Blockunvir hesitated, then heaved a breath like a dragon and sat on one of the cushions beside the table. "Verily, you are wise, shopkeeper." He glanced around, his hand drifting towards the hilt of his battle ax slung across his shoulders. "Yet my wolf-keen senses tell me we are not alone."

Igvore sat cross-legged on the other side of the table. "That would be Thronk, bringing tea."

On cue, the Silent Giant swept through another curtained doorway with a silver platter. He'd chosen the teapot with a hydra painted on it, and two delicate porcelain cups with saucers. That was Igvore's favorite pot: the spout looked like a dragon head and breathed steam. A fresh plate of warm gingerbread cookies, a bowl of sugared dates, and a small pitcher of cream finished off the tray.

Thronk beamed, set everything down, and proceeded to pour the fragrant tea for both Blockunvir and Igvore. Then he quickly signed, *I've got to finish the zucchini bread batter and pop the apple crisp into the oven. Enjoy!*

"Thank you, Thronk! Help yourself," Igvore said to Blockunvir. "I don't know how that man has so many talents, but by the gods, I promise you have *never* had cookies like the kind Thronk bakes. It's an open secret that every third night he works as a short-order cook at Eggplants and Oysters. The veggie gyros were his creation."

"Mmmhmmf," Blockunvir said, pushing a third cookie into his mouth, chewing furiously.

Igvore beamed. They always got vicarious pleasure through people enjoying Thronk's cooking.

"So." Igvore sipped their tea and nibbled on a cookie. The perfect amount of cinnamon, clove, and sweet molasses in a chewy center with crisped edges. "Tell me what troubles you."

Blockunvir shifted restlessly, then ate another cookie. "'Tis a strange thing, shopkeeper. For when I hunt in the land of dreams, 'tis not great ogres and hydras that I battle! I see oft strange halls, hung with tapestries of gold and ruby, with the skins of bears upon the hearth and myself wielding not a blade but..." His face flushed and he waved a hand, spraying crumbs. "By Grimfang, 'tis not important! Any sage would tell me 'tis but the restlessness of idle hands. Verily, there be not a beast in sight within these dream-walls—I have sought soothsayers and seers, and yet none can decipher this riddle of the night."

Igvore considered, tapping the lip of their teacup. "In my own adventuring days," they said, "I traveled often with a sorceress whose power lay in the dreams of those around her." They smiled wistfully. Those had been good days, if stressful. "She taught me much of her technique. Actually, it was through her training that I was able to foresee my own path as a small business owner."

"Who was this mighty sage?" Blockunvir demanded, leaning forward.

"Goveria Goremonger—you might know of her as the famed Black Pearl of the Void? Well, she retired shortly after I did, and now she designs a very successful and practical, pocket-friendly fashion line." Igvore dipped a hand into their overcoat pocket to demonstrate.

"By Attormok's flaming nostrils!"

Igvore nodded in agreement. "Goveria has been very successful, and I'm forever grateful to her for guiding my fate this way."

Igvore had made their theatrical debut in the saga *Flashing Blade, Rippling Steel* as Nameless Grunt Three. They'd traveled with several different troubadours but ultimately found their interests swayed towards actual quests and perilous adventuring as a rare barbarian-bard. Goveria and Igvore had met in a tavern brawl, after which she'd invited them to join her, and following many epic sagas, the pair had parted ways, and history marched into the pages of time.

"Lest you think my experience limited," Igvore went on, for while they rarely bragged about their clientele or past exploits, they'd never lost their flair for dramatics. It helped in the customer service industry. "Covar the Conqueror is also a former client of mine."

Blockunvir's eyes widened. "Ipthash's mighty thighs! *The* Covar? Hero of the Wastefall Rebellion? He who slew the unstoppable winterdrakes and ended the Reign of Ice?"

"The same Covar, although they recently came out as agender and use the pronouns they/them."

Blockunvir whistled in awe. "I thought they were lost to the abyssal plane years ago!"

"A slight detour, as they like to put it," Igvore chuckled. "Anyway, yes, they consulted with me and eventually they opened a retirement home for magical and soul-bound weapons. They've also taken to gardening. Biggest pumpkins you've ever seen come from Covar's patch!"

The massive barbarian sipped his tea, his gaze wistful now. "'Tis been a long while since I tasted good pumpkin ale."

"Season for it is coming up," Igvore said.

They wondered if Kassdara was preparing for the inevitable hauntings that would beset Covar's pumpkins. Kassdara, along with her wife—the famed alchemist Sonya Carmella Nightshadebane—experimented in making micro-beers from exotic and de-possessed plantlife. Igvore always looked forward to invitations to beer tastings with anticipation, though they prepared by painting exorcism wards along their throat and belly before drinking anything Kassdara and her wife served.

Modestly, Igvore motioned to the back wall, where they'd had the scrolls and parchments of successful business deeds and praise from old clients framed in preservation spells for posterity.

"I have many more references I am happy to share, but let's return to your needs, friend. You mentioned not wielding a blade in your dreams," Igvore said. "I swear upon my blood that what you choose to tell me will not leave this room. What is it you see in dreams?"

Blockunvir worked his jaw, as if chewing over the possibility of revealing the deepest knowledge of his soul. "'Tis needles I see," the barbarian said under his breath. "Knitting needles."

"Oh, that's wonderful! What do you like making?" Igvore asked.

Blockunvir blinked several times, taken aback. "This does not... diminish thine view of me?"

"Never, Blockunvir," Igvore said. "Knitting is a noble and long-lived tradition among warriors. I could recommend some pattern shops, if you like?"

"Grimfang's beard," Blockunvir said, looking rather dazed. "I have told naught a living soul of this..."

"It's a *wonderful* skill," Igvore said, flushed with exhilaration. "Do you see yourself knitting to sell, or more as a personal hobby?"

"The socks are, uh... mine toes did near freeze when I traversed the arctic tors of Veynwean. Yet no shopkeep I sought sold proper stockings for the boots they had in plenty." Blockunvir tugged at a lock of his hair that had come untwined from the hair stick. "In truth, the tapestries in my dreams are ones made by mine own hand... yet on a loom."

"Oh, excellent," Igvore said. "So multiple textile products? Socks are an absolute necessity, although you may wish to consider closed-toed shoes instead of sandals?"

"Do you take me for a heathen?" Blockunvir suddenly roared, his mighty sinews standing out like cords on his neck.

Igvore held up their hands in supplication. "Sorry, that was callus of me. I beg your forgiveness."

The barbarian simmered, but then smiled sheepishly. "They are comfortable when in private, though..."

"Absolutely," Igvore agreed—and not a little relieved that Blockunvir's wrath was more for show. They did so hate having one-on-one combat in the tearoom. It made such a mess. "And I swear by my nice pair of voidlamb slippers—like small pools of darkness to engulf your feet."

"By Angrok's single eye, verily!" Blockunvir said, slapping his thigh. "'Tis not nearly enough heed paid to such luxuries."

Igvore nodded. "Tell me, friend. Have you considered establishing your own business?"

Blockunvir furrowed his brow, glancing around again as if spied upon by devious enemies. "Nay?"

"Running your own business is not for everyone, true," Igvore said. "But it occurs to me, if knitting and weaving are your desires, perhaps you could set up a shop in the vicinity. I would be more than happy to stock your products, considering I now realize I do not have any kind of stockings or slippers in my inventory..."

Blockunvir stroked his chin, gazing into the distance as his barbarian mind turned over the implications and possibilities.

"Plus," Igvore added slyly, "I think Thronk would like to see you again."

Blockunvir's jaw fell open. "He—he would? But how would you know?"

"Call it a hunch," Igvore said, and winked. "It's not every customer he eyes that way."

Blockunvir's face turned as flame-hued as his hair. "I have faced eldritch horrors beyond the ken of mortal minds but 'twould not have the courage to, uh... well."

"Ask him out?"

Blockunvir nodded.

"Don't worry," Igvore said. "I can help with that. I'll bring you to the Eggplant and Oysters tonight. Thronk is cooking, and he does love sharing his veggie gyros."

"My thanks, shopkeeper—you have more than earned your pay!" Blockunvir reached to his coin pouch, but Igvore waved him off.

"Look, think about what I said," Igvore went on. "If it's a new quest into entrepreneurship you seek, I'm happy to connect you with local yarn and wool sellers. You've revealed to me a market need that must be met. This could be the start of an adventurous partnership."

"'Tis settled!" Blockunvir proclaimed. He thrust his hand out, and Igvore shook the barbarian's massive paw. Then he leaned in and whispered, "You were not jesting about, uh, introducing me to the Silent Giant?"

"I never jest about my clients' happiness," Igvore said. "Let us finish our tea, and I will draw up some letters of recommendation to suppliers in the area, if you wish to explore different options."

They were satisfied that regardless if Blockunvir took up knitting with the same vigor as he slew monsters, he would know he was always welcome in the Loincloth and the Broadsword.

HEXPOCOLYPSE

1

"The hex washes off, dude, relax." Steven stuck his tongue out in concentration as he drew on my bicep. "It's gonna be so awesome[1]."

"Right," I said. "So unbelievably cool you couldn't try it on yourself first?"

"Shut up and hold still," Steven said.

Permanent marker scraped against my skin. It wasn't the worst smell in the classroom, but ever since the incident of putting magic ink in a microwave to see what would happen, I didn't like the odor.

---

[1] CN: crude humor, fantasy violence, attempted violence against students by a teacher, verbal abuse, violence against (immortal) fish, minor gore, self-harm behavior

Around us, the fourth year cursers watched at a safe distance. This was *not* how I imagined getting in on the good side of Steven and his clique. I was skeptical this was even an official hazing ritual. Besides being the test subject for the Most Forbidden Hex Ever that *I'd* stolen from the headmaster, the smell of marker ink was making me queasy.

"There!" Steven held up my arm so everyone could see.

The appropriate "ooohs," "wicked," and "aaaahs" sounded on cue. I still didn't know if Steven had a spell on his forehead that prompted the right responses to whatever he did on cue, but his friends never missed a beat. Either that or they rehearsed like hell to get it right during non-class hours.

I peered at new hex.

It looked like the Horus Eye had gotten pwned by an ankh through the pupil, and in Steven's creative cursive script, triple sixes arched above the signs.

Steven capped the marker and tossed it on Mr. Hendershall's desk. Our geometry teacher lay zoned out behind the desk. He always took a nap the first half of the period. I was pretty sure it was because he was a were-sloth.

Rudie, Steven's best friend and right-hand guy, whistled. "So, you figure out what it does, Steve-o?"

I gaped at Steven. "You don't know what it *does*?"

Steven rolled his eyes. "There weren't any instructions on the grimoire or explanation on what it means. But it's awesome. And we'll find out."

I wanted to run away screaming but I didn't want to wake Mr. Hendershall early and get back to work on chapter six—pentagrams. So I sat on the edge of the teacher's desk and waited with everyone else.

We all looked at my arm.

Nothing happened.

Steven picked up the grimoire I'd nicked out of the headmaster's safe box when he was in a conference call. That's what I was good at: snatching stuff. No one really knew why. I just... sort of did it.

Yeah, it's great for getting third helpings of Mom's cherry-double-chocolate-chip-fudge brownies she guards in the fridge with triplicate defense wards, but there's this thing called a conscience. I used to think my immortal pet goldfish Natasha was my conscience, since she would bombard me telepathically with Warnings About the Evils of Sin, and repent now and all will be forgiven, blah blah blah.

I'd flushed her down the toilet after the fourth sermon in the middle of watching Broomstick Massacre IV. She came back. I thanked the god she kept babbling about that she couldn't heft an ax when she flopped up the stairs and burst into my bedroom. Well, squeezed under the door and railed at me until I put her back in the fishbowl. Still. It was creepy.

Anyway, the whole conscience thing, it was a pain in the butt. I had this idea stealing was wrong. But I'd gone and gotten the Unspoken Warlock's

Grimoire and handed it over to Steven. Because he'd said that was what I had to do to join his group of cool kids.

Rudie jabbed me in the arm below the hex. "Dude, nothing is happening."

"Ow," I said. "Watch it. It could explode."

Rudie took a hasty step backwards. I really hoped it wouldn't explode.

Steven flipped through the pages written in blood while some of the guys started a spitball fight. Someone had learned how to make neon orange phlegm. I'd have loved to join in—I mean, can you imagine how sweet glow in the dark yellow snot would be?—but I felt something twitch in my arm.

"Whoa!" Steven pointed at me, and the spitball war paused with globs of neon saliva hung in the air.

I was the first brave soldier to breach the silence as everyone stared at Steven. "What?"

"Um." Steven went pale. I mean, not just that vampiric-and-doesn't-get-enough-sunlight-pale.

I mean scared-out-of-your-frigging-mind pale. "Guys?"

We all leaned toward him.

"We, um, we just sort of..."

My arm sparked. I jumped. "What the heck!" The hex hadn't changed, so I looked at Steven. "C'mon, man, what's going on?"

Steven showed us the page of the grimoire he'd been reading. The picture of the hex was on it. Next to the drawing there was one word written in English, French, Spanish, spellese, and Egyptian hieroglyphics, just like those multi-lingual instruction manuals you get with electronics.

Except the word was Armageddon.

"Dude," I said. "We just started the apocalypse?"

2.

"How did you not see that before you started drawing?" I whisper-yelled.

"The text only just showed up now!" Steven snapped, his voice squeakier then mine.

A trumpet sounded. It wasn't coming from music study hall, either. It sounded like it was in the sky, and I'd heard Natasha rail passages of Revelations at me enough to have a guess what that trumpet was.

"Crap, man," I said, looking at Steven.

"Hey, dude, it's on *your* arm," he said. "*You* stole the book. This is so your problem." He shoved the grimoire at me and then on that unseen cue I wasn't synced up with, the other guys scattered.

I was alone in Mr. Hendershall's classroom, in the the Orange County School for Warlocks, holding the most forbidden tome ever, and the sky outside was blackening faster than my sister Zoe's attempts at cooking bacon.

Crack! Boom! Crackle!

I dived under the desk as the windows shook. From this angle, I was watching Mr. Hendershall still doing unconscious yoga on the floor behind his desk.

"Mr. Göttenal!" a voice boomed, and it was coming from inside the classroom. It was the headmaster.

I jumped, smacked my head so hard my brains almost came out my ears, and imagined myself invisible. The cloaking spells always ended up making my skin invisible and the rest of me not. The walking X-ray thing was cool for all of five seconds before everyone got grossed out.

"Mr. Göttenal, where are you!"

I suspect that all students are fitted with these brain controlling devices when they're born to respond to That Tone the headmaster used. You can't decide, "Nah, screw it, I'm not coming out now," because you have to. Or maybe the threat of detention just scares everyone with a brain. I know it scared me. School was an escape from the family and the zombie experiments in the basement. Oh, and Natasha of course.

I came out.

The headmaster wasn't old, I mean, not like my grandpa. He looked maybe just out of college, in his sweater and kakis and slicked back hair.

Rumor had it he was nine-hundred. I'd say maybe a few days over twenty-five. He had his clipboard in hand and his gecko familiar sitting on his shoulder. They both wore protective goggles. He pushed his up on his forehead and scowled at me.

"Yes, sir?" I said.

The headmaster has Timing. I don't mean just knowing when to walk into a classroom to catch you stealing answers off someone else's tests with spell hooks, or apprehending smoking in the bathrooms, or walking in on illegal spelling on school property. No, I mean when he stormed in, pissed off, and saw me standing there with hex on my arm, grimoire in hand, and the sky is raining dead angels—

Wait. What?

The cracks outside, which had sounded like thunderclaps or meteors breaking wind in the atmosphere, weren't what they seemed. Something white, feathery, and not a seagull rocketed past the window. No, that wasn't a riddle.

BOOM.

The impact rattled the wards and glass window panes.

The headmaster rubbed the goggle marks under his eyes. "Give me the grimoire."

I offered it to him.

He pulled. The book stayed attached to my hand. Not with tentacles like the reincarnated math textbook that one time in First Year. It wouldn't let him take it. I tried dropping it on the floor, and it growled at me.

I swallowed. "Um, I don't think it's going to work, sir."

"I can see that, Mr. Göttenal." The headmaster eyeballed me. So did his gecko. "We can try cutting off your hand and surgically reattaching it but I'll need a note of consent from your parents."

The grimoire snarled louder.

"I don't think it likes that idea, sir."

A gray-feathered angel plummeted past the window and this time the glass cracked when it made impact. Pretty soon the defensive wards that prevented meteors from hitting the school buildings wouldn't be so deflective. I cleared my throat. "Maybe we should evacuate?"

"I have a better idea," the headmaster said. He pointed his clipboard at me. "Come, Mr. Göttenal." He turned around and stormed down the hall.

I followed. Every time I tugged at the grimoire, it stuck harder to me. "Where are we going, sir?"

We navigated the halls now absent of the usual chaos of other students. I hadn't heard the lockdown alarms over the noise outside.

"Shouldn't we head to the safe zones, sir?"

"Oh, we are."

I didn't know there was a safe zone on the roof, just the helicopter and broom landing pads.

The grimoire sat heavy and warm and almost fuzzy on my hand. My arm kept itching where the hex was. Didn't Steven say it would wash off?

"Uh, sir," I said, "shouldn't we try to remove the hex with soap and water first?"

He opened the door to the fire escape and motioned me to follow him up onto the roof. It had dropped to freezing temperatures outside.

Snowstorms in May might have been usual for my Uncle Vottenhiemer, when his cows started messing with the weather patterns, but here in Florida I don't think anyone appreciated the sudden blizzard.

I shivered as snowflakes, angel feathers, and a bass rumbling boom hit me full in the face. I squinted and wiped at my eyes with the hand *not* occupied by an ancient cursed spellbook.

The headmaster put up a casual heat wave around us, and the melted snow dripped off his bubble as we climbed the fire escape.

On the roof, he motioned me to look towards the bay.

Holy mothballs from Aunt Susan's closet.

There was a Leviathan in the bay, and it looked hungry.

3.

The Leviathan was purplish gray, with a thick neck and huge mouth and its breath smelled like garlic and fish even from a distance. I gagged and covered my nose. "What are we doing here?"

I looked around for the safe zone, but there weren't any wards, or lead-lined rooms, or even a straw barricade.

The headmaster clapped a hand on my shoulder. "Did you read the grimoire before getting the hex mark on your arm, Mr. Göttenal?"

Of course not. I wasn't one of those über-geeks who wrote their thesis before even graduating seventh year. "No, sir."

"I'll paraphrase for you."

The headmaster muttered a phrase in Old Spelivan and my arms stuck to my sides, grimoire and everything. It was worse than the superglue and rice paper incident, which honestly wasn't my fault.

"Hey!" I said. "Not cool!" I squirmed and tried to get my arms to move. I failed epically.

The headmaster watched me. His gecko rolled its eyes. "The fastest way to reverse a hexpocolypse is to destroy the hex."

"Hexpocolypse?" It might have been a sweet word under normal circumstances. Right now, I wasn't interested in a dictionary definition. "Destroy?"

"Yes, Mr. Göttenal. And the wearer."

Seriously. Not. Cool. I gaped at him as my feet left the ground and his spell lifted me over the helicopter pad and flung me out towards the bay. "Wait a minute, Steven said it washes off with soap and water!"

"Amusing."

"How the hell do you know this!" Caution: voice entering high-pitch break mode. Level orange. Proceed with care.

"Mr. Göttenal," the headmaster said, turning his back on me. His spell was on autopilot. "I am always prepared for student pranks and idiocy. Including initiation of a hexpocolypse."

Think, Boris, I told myself as the binding spell ferried me over the school grounds, past the access road and broom parking lot, and closer to the bay.

Oh, crap!

The Leviathan opened its mouth wide, blackish tongue sweeping out even longer and more disgusting than a Newfoundland's. I bet sea monster drool was worse than dog slobber, too.

There was no way I could break the headmaster's binding spell—I didn't know Old Spelivan, for one thing. And I was fifty feet in the air, so even if I *did* wiggle out, I'd have to get a flotation bubble around myself double-fast or it would be Boris-splatter all over the ground.

My sister would find that hilarious and Natasha would have a fire and brimstone sermon for me on the nature of suicide. For a moment, I wondered if Mom would bring me back as a zombie.

No, probably not.

I wasn't going splat if I had anything to say about it. If gravity wanted my opinion, it sucked, and I didn't play by the rules all the time.

I came up with a brilliant, masterminded genius plan: which was to scream my head off. Nothing like panic to exercise the developing lungs in non-jock stock students. I bet that was the driving philosophy behind physical ed.

So I did that until I noticed the mines on the beach.

Words like "boom", "flying body parts", and "excruciating pain" bounced through my head. I'd survived gym class already today. What were a few warlock-planted sensor mines that could rip you to pieces, right?

It was risk that or become monster chow.

Concentrating, I peered down and then kicked off one of my shoes. It flopped through the air and then landed smack in the middle of one of the mines.

BOOM!

WHAM!

"AHHHHHHH!"

That last one was *not* me, I swear.

The shockwave slammed into me with a sidedish of sand and shrapnel. I went spinning in acrobatic circles back the way I'd come, and my lunch almost came out my nose. I screamed and squeezed my eyes shut.

The grimoire slammed into my chest, though I wasn't quite sure how it did that. My arms were still glued to my sides.

"GRRRRRR," the grimoire said, and it sounded pissed off.

There was a snap-pop-fizz and then the headmaster's binding went bye-bye.

And I went speeding headfirst towards a the parking lot.

4.

"*Floatius*!" I shouted. "*Featherius*! Blast it, *float*!"

I couldn't remember the proper wording for a levitation spell. Admittedly, I was kind of lazy in the "studying for tests and doing homework" department.

I could see individual grains of tar through the tunnel vision before I got the spell right. "*Floatation heliumius*!"

I suddenly became lighter than the air around me. Hah, suck it, gravity!

Impact hurt anyway, and I pitied basketballs.

Bouncing several times and doing an impressive barrel roll a few inches above the broken tarmac, I at last cut the spell and landed face-first on the gravelly side of the road.

"Ow."

"Mweh?"

"Huh?" My eyes were still doing pirouettes in my skull. I blinked hard and squinted up at the thing staring back at me.

"Mweh?" it said again, looking at me with a couple dozen eyes.

"Aaah!"

I scrambled up. The flawless backflip into a running sprint that would have been worthy of competition in the Warlock Olympics got a 2.0 for execution. I jumped up, my head spun, and I fell on my butt.

The creature staring at me might have been cute if it didn't have all those eyeballs. Cute in a it'll-grow-up-and-bring-you-to-your-doom kinda way. It was a lion cub with six chubby wings, all studded with wide blue kitten eyes. It might have been golden-white, like my favorite yellow shirt that got bleach rained on it, but it kept shimmering as if not quite grounded in our reality.

Don't get me started on reality grounding. Dad had a book-length lecture on the subject he'd given me when I'd tried to slip out of the space-time continuum to avoid a math quiz.

"Mweh?" the apocalyptic beastie asked me, toddling forward. It tripped over its front feet and flopped on its face, wings fluttering in a babyish, clumsy circles.

"Aww, hey little thing. What the heck are you, huh?"

It purred.

I scooped it up and set it back on its feet; it was, maybe predictably, lighter than a feather. I used one hand, the other attached once more to the grimoire, and felt the book growl jealously. I ignored it. The winged lion cub looked up at me. I rubbed it under the chin.

The crackling sonic boom and smell of burnt ozone warned me too late of a falling angel. It impacted off the side of the road and the shockwave sent me and the lion cub flying across the ditch.

We landed in a heap with it sitting on my chest. The sky was turning darker and darker and flashes of red lightning and frothy pink storm clouds in the east were giving it the whole Ominous Appearance.

In the bay, the Leviathan bellowed and splashed, sending a mini tidal wave at the school grounds. We were far enough away to get a light sprinkling and nothing more. The burning feather smell and the smoke from the angel crater burned my eyes, and I decided it was high time to get the heck out of there.

Pretty soon the headmaster would realize the Leviathan hadn't eaten me for a high protein, low carb snack and would come looking for me. He took his whole Duty and Responsibility and Sacrificing Innocent Students to Monsters very seriously.

I scooped up the lion cub, whom I named Doomkitty on the spot, and ran for home.

It was nearly pitch black when I finished dodging the chaos that wasn't the usual highway traffic. I raced up the driveway, hoping no one had forgotten any time bombs on the gravel again.

Today the house was a gingerbread Victorian mansion painted plum and gold, with white trim and a lime green roof—I wasn't sure if that was mold or just a paint-job on the shingles.

Dad's degree in theoretical astrophysics and quantum reality manipulation wasn't all that theoretical when it came to changing our house. Things inside our rooms and personal possessions stayed the same. Luckily, after Mom threatened to make Dad sleep on the street when he tried the Mesopotamian adobe with mud-brick walls and a hole where the toilet had been, he now stuck to designs that accommodated all the necessities in life, like electricity and plumbing and fiber internet.

Okay, time to wash off the hex and restore my life to normal. I shouldered my way inside with

Doomkitty in tow, all its eyes blinking. A formula in the quantum housing design code allowed all family members and pets to know exactly where everything was in a new layout. So I sidetracked to the kitchen for some of the heavier duty cleaning solution.

There were zombies in the kitchen again.

I scowled at them. I had bigger worries—like the end of the world—than raiding the cookie jar. But I still didn't need to deal with dead skin flakes and dirt being tracked on the floor when it was my turn to clean the kitchen.

"Get out!" I slapped at them with the grimoire and they moaned and shuffled out.

"Boris?"

Crap. I couldn't let my sister see the hex, and if she was texting her friends, or watching the news, she'd probably heard about the apocalypse going on. And since kid sisters are like that, she'd think it was *my* fault and tell Mom and Dad.

Not what I needed.

"No one's here," I said, and sprinted for my room.

5.

I raced up three—yes, three—flights of stairs, down the hall, and found my bedroom behind the last room on the left. There were gas lamps along the hall, and the door had six panels and a lion-headed knocker that growled at me.

I held up Doomkitty, who hissed, and the knocker whimpered and the door swung open. Racing inside, I dropped the winged lion kitten on the bed and looked around for Natasha. Sometimes she cloaked her fishbowl, though I wasn't sure if was an *actual* cloaking device or just a trick she picked up.

Natasha wasn't in sight, but I spotted her fishbowl near the window, tipped on its side, and all the water soaking my latest issue of *Wonder Witch,* a new comic series I'd started reading last week. Now that just wasn't fair.

While the walls were a dull wooden paneling, all my posters of Rolling Warlocks were still in place. The usual junk, old food wrappers, dirty clothes, and all the comforts of a guy's room were just how I'd left them.

Except there was a red-skinned demon sitting on my dresser. He couldn't have been two feet in height, and he had goat legs crossed under him, a human-like chest and not very impressive pecs, a long pointed tail, and horns above his ears. Pretty much the typical cliché you'd see in cartoons, except he was dressed in black leather, chains, and had an electric guitar resting on his lap.

And he was totally using my iPod.

Talk about gross—I wasn't wearing those ear buds again after he'd stuck them in his ears. Earwax was bad enough, but hellish earwax?

"Okay, that's it." Getting almost fed to a Leviathan, adopting an apocalyptic symbol (even a baby one), and finding zombies in the kitchen was bad enough, but *no one* touched my iPod. "Give that to me right now!"

The demon jumped so high his horns lodged in the ceiling and he hung there. He dropped his guitar, too, and a string popped loose. "Holy water, don't sneak up on an imp like that!"

He tugged one horn free, then the other, and landed with a *thunk* on the dresser again, knocking over my fake trophy I'd gotten to fool Dad into thinking I won something in sports, and my alarm clock with the animated rooster head. The clock cock-a-doodle-doo'd until I stomped on its head.

"Give me my iPod."

The imp clutched it and eyed me. "It's mine now."

I gaped at him. "Dude, it's got my name engraved on it."

"Mine."

"Mine," I said.

"Nope." He stood, did a taunting dance that left hoof prints on the lacquered dresser, and then frolicked across the wall in kung-fu movie style and headed for the door.

Who doesn't like a game of chasing the annoying imp from hell around the transdimensional house? Greatest entertainment since reality TV.

I yelled words Mom would have a fit about if she heard them and chased the imp. It didn't occur to me until the imp slid down the curved banister and left burn marks with his tail that I'd have to explain why there was a demon romping around with my iPod. I decided on playing it clueless—I mean, I didn't really *know* why he was here anyway, right?

I puffed down the last few stairs, but the imp had disappeared.

In the living room/parlor, my sister was planted in front of the plasma TV. Planted, literally, as in she had roots. Mom had decided she wasn't getting enough sun since she wouldn't play outside, so she genetically implanted some hibiscus genes into Zoe. Don't get me wrong, having a mad scientist for a mom is cool and all, in the right circles, but sometimes the moral of Doctor Frankenstein comes to mind.

Zoe glanced at me, flowers and leaves sprouting out of her head. She was mostly still a girl, except for the feet merged into a stalk with roots and the petals instead of hair. Mom had promised to fix it tomorrow when she got the subatomic gene manipulator fixed after one of the zombies slobbered on it.

"Did a two foot tall bright red imp run by here?" I asked Zoe, too mad about my iPod to care about staying subtle.

Zoe rolled her fuchsia colored eyes. She'd ordered them off late night infomercials. I still thought they looked tacky.

"Do I look like I saw something like—aaaaaahhh!"

I spun around, and saw the imp dancing around the hallway, waggling his butt at me.

"My eyes, my eyes!" Zoe cried. "Get it out of my sight, Boris, it has no fashion sense!" Then she snickered. "You're such a weirdo, bro. Just don't let Mom catch you with that thing."

I ran and grabbed at the demon. He ran up the walls and pulled a face at me from the ceiling.

"Give me my iPod, you little creep!" I shouted.

Suddenly the imp froze, his face pulled into a horrified look. His horns stabbed through the hallway rug and he slumped over backwards, grimacing.

I reached over and yanked my iPod out of his hand and the ear buds as well.

Something bulged and writhed in his stomach, pressing against his skin.

"Whoa. Don't do an *Alien* on me here, dude." I backed up a safe distance, and raised the grimoire in front of my face, but low enough I could still peek over.

The imp clutched his stomach and shrieked, fire and smoke puffing from his mouth. It set off the sprinkler system. I got drenched, Zoe screamed she was being over-watered, and the water snuffed out the fire and so the imp started coughing up steam instead.

And then Natasha exploded out of his stomach.

6.

The imp screamed louder than I did, but Zoe still beat us both by at least three octaves and maybe a hundred decibels.

What's gray and red and gold all over? One mad as hell immortal goldfish with imp innards on her scales. I've always hated jokes like that.

I lunged forward and caught Natasha. She slipped and flopped in my hands, but I had the presence of mind to stomp on the imp's tail before he could scurry off. He just lay there, wailing, and the din was bound to attract Mom or Dad's attention. Eventually. But I didn't want to risk it if I didn't have to.

"Shut up, all of you!" I yelled.

Blasphemy! Natasha screeched telepathically. Get thee behind me, Satan!

"He's too low on the infernal ladder to count, Natty." I cupped her in my palm, and the grimoire growled. She quoted a passage from Revelations at it and gave it the evil eye.

"It's getting guts on the floor," Zoe said, folding her petals and scrunching up her nose. "Boys are so gross."

A massive crash sounded outside and the sidewalk alarms blared Beethoven's Fifth. It used to be "Night on Bald Mountain," but my dad had issues with that composer after meeting his clone once.

Why burglars were headed for us, I didn't know, and it seemed fairly insignificant.

"Everyone shut up and listen to me." I stomped on the imp's tail for emphasis.

He shrieked.

"Zoe, do we have any superglue?" I asked, holding onto Natasha as she spouted verses from Job.

"Kitchen drawer." Zoe returned to watching her show. "Keep it down, will you?"

I didn't know any imp or demon binding spells, but there was that summer drama camp I'd been taken to in a case of mistaken identity, and the improv helped now. "Spawn the devil, I bind thee with my will! Thou wilt, uh, be bound to my service and voice."

"Are you kidding me?" the imp sat up, holding his guts in and gave me a withering look.

"No." I glared back. "You do what I say or I'll feed you to Doomkitty."

Said incarnation of holy wrath and fiendish appetite had waddled down the hall and now hid behind my leg.

"Mweh?"

I sighed.

I couldn't just leave the imp to run around the house wrecking havoc. Well, I *could*. But I'd get grounded for life if Mom found out.

"I'll patch up your stomach if you do what I say, how's that?" I said.

"Get the glue," the imp said, sulking.

"Watch him, Doomkitty. If he moves, eat him."

"Mrow."

I dashed into the kitchen, glad the zombies were gone. I dropped Natasha in a half-filled mug of cold coffee where she railed at me about the lusts of the flesh and the evils of caffeine addiction. I grabbed a Coke out of the fridge just to mock her and gulped down two huge swallows. I hadn't realized how thirsty bringing about a hexpocolypse and almost dying could make you.

“Drawers” were not lacking in the new layout. I guessed at random and after ten different tries, I found a tube of Mom’s homemade zombie limb and intestine adhesive.

The grimoire was an endless means of building character, like not cursing in frustration when it hampered the opening drawers and the sorting through possessed handheld beaters, opera singing timers, and bespelled measuring cups.

I banged my funny bone on a counter edge and danced around, wincing.

“Look.” I held up my arm to glare at the grimoire. “I’d really appreciate it if you could stick somewhere else, okay? It’s not like I’m going to leave you lying around. I need you, you need me. Can’t we work something out?”

Grudgingly, the grimoire unstuck my arm and I considered where to place it. I sighed and slapped it on my chest, where it clung possessively.

“Thanks.” It never hurt to be polite to ancient tomes of unspeakable evil.

I snatched the coffee mug, since I didn't trust Natasha out of my sight just now, and ran back to the hallway.

The imp was gone. Doomkitty looked up at me with sad eyes—yes, all of them—and its six wings drooped. I slapped my forehead. "Where'd he go?"

A cackling from the dining room answered that question. He was smearing butter on his hooves and "ice skating" across the polished tabletop, leaving blackened skid marks on the maple finish. His stomach, I noted, was closed up and he somehow had my iPod again.

I slammed Natasha's mug down so hard she splashed out. She landed on the floor and found Doomkitty looking down at her with that typical cat-like stare of hungry fascination.

"Don't eat her," I warned Doomkitty.

Natasha launched into her sermon about the "thou shalt not kill" commandment.

I had an imp to murder in the name of my iPod.

"Yaaaaaaah!" I hurled myself at him with a little boosting spell I was officially forbidden to use in the house after I'd knocked Zoe into next week. It was totally an accident, I swear.

The imp bounced toward the ceiling, but I expected it this time and modified my trajectory. I slammed into him, grabbed him around the neck, and we both crashed onto the table.

He slapped me in the face. I picked him up and dribbled him like a basketball on the floor before resuming the chokehold.

"I've had it, you little devil," I said. "Give me your name, rank, and serial number or whatever the the equivalent is, and tell me what you're doing in my house. And do it now!"

"Never!" The imp grinned in defiance. "You're running out of time and I'll never talk. Do your worst, human mortal."

No more mister nice hexified Boris. He wanted me to bring out the heavy artillery, I'd bring it out. I grabbed for Natasha.

"Talk," I said, dangling the ranting, glowering, lip-gnashing Natasha over the demon's face. "Or I'll sic the goldfish on you."

The imp's eyes bulged and he whimpered. "Okay, okay!"

"You swear to do what I say?" I lowered Natasha towards his nose.

"Yes, I swear! Keep that thing away from me!"

"Swear it."

"I swear."

"Swear it!"

"I swear, thrice sworn to the mortal born. Done. Oh please, not the goldfish..."

There was a click-snap in my brain and the grimoire gave an approving growl.

I let the imp go. "Give my iPod and don't touch it again."

He handed it over. Without the battery.

"Where's the..."

He grinned and rubbed his stomach.

"Never mind." The music outside increased in tempo and Doomkitty shivered and pressed against my leg.

"Who are you and what are you doing here?" I rubbed my head. "Talk on the way, I have a hex to wash off."

7.

I tucked Natasha back in the mug, then with the imp and Doomkitty in tow, I marched for the upstairs bathroom. For one thing, that had a lock with a retina scanner so I could keep Zoe out as well as any wandering zombies.

"I'm Greg," the imp said.

I looked over my shoulder. He swaggered along, the winged lion now as tall as he was. I blinked. Doomkitty had doubled in size, and looked less cute and more holy warrior avenger-ish, in a kitten sort of way.

"Greg?" I asked.

"Gregoriantentatocolius."

"Greg works."

"I'm here to offer you a deal." Greg's hooves clicked the hardwood floor. "Since you have the Mark, you can get a discount on high ranking positions when the Master shows up."

"Discounts?"

"Well, you only need to pay a quarter of your soul up front," Greg said. "And the second quarter when you're named the Beast's right hand... kid. So it's a great deal—all the benefits of unlimited power for only half your soul!"

I eyed him while I simultaneously scanned my retina and the bathroom door swung open. "Only half my soul?"

"Bargain of an eternal lifetime!" Greg leaned forward. "I can get you a sweet deal on—"

"No thanks. Is that all you're here for?"

"I need the book." He pointed at the grimoire latched onto my chest. "Well, my Master does. I'm just the messenger."

"Why does he need the book?" I dropped Natasha in the sink, ignoring her rants about sin and temptation and downfalls, and ushered them all in, then shut and locked the door. "I mean, obviously it's evil and all and maybe it'd make a good souvenir, but..."

"Oh, so no one can reverse things before six hours."

"What do you mean, six hours?"

Greg gripped his horns and then slammed his head into the door. "Crap, I wasn't supposed to tell you that!"

"Hey, you agreed to do what I say. And stop that, you're denting the woodwork." I frowned. "Now answer me, Greg. What do you mean by six hours?"

Greg sat down and picked unidentifiable stuff from between his cloven hooves. "Once the Mark is inscribed, it can't be removed after six hours. All this—" He waved a hand, and I hoped he meant the dead angels and Leviathan and everything else outside, not my bathroom. "—is just the tremors before the big quake, if you know what I mean." He winked at me.

I stopped wasting time and rooted around under the sink for the bottle with the poison sticker marked "industrial cleaning solution." I hoped it didn't take off more than just permanent marker. I might not have a lot of muscles, but I do like to keep the ones I have. I'd seen some of

Mom's concoctions melt zombies, and she was horrible at not marking containers properly.

So I poured some of the bubbling, hissing solution on a towel and tested it on Greg's horn.

He jumped, screeching at the top of his lungs, but he didn't melt into goo or spontaneously combust. His horn just looked shinier.

"Relax," I said. "It's just soap."

"Are you *kidding* me?" Greg screamed. "Soap? Do you know how long I've avoided having a bath? Three hundred years, kid! Aaaaarrggh!"

"Jeez, I'm sorry." I shrugged. "Wash it off."

"No water! I'm a fiery imp from Hell! I don't do water!"

"Okay, okay!" I rolled my eyes and looked at the sticky towel. The soap, if that's what it really was, had turned the blue towel a sickly green. The grimoire quivered and growled on my chest, and I swear it was trying to poke me.

"Here goes nothing," I muttered and dabbed the towel on my arm. "OW!"

It stung worse than a swarm of genetically engineered wasps. I danced around the small bathroom, yelping. That got Greg shrieking about getting infected by the towel I waved around, Natasha bellowed another sermon, and Doomkitty started crying—which sounded like a baby roar now.

A fist pounded on the door. "Boris, what are you doing?"

We all froze.

It was Mom.

Some people might think having an evil mad scientist for a mom is pretty cool. Sometimes the living brownies or the killer chocolate chip cookies were pretty awesome to bring to class, but there were downsides too, like avoiding being her next guinea pig.

Added to that, Mom's work wasn't strictly legal. The whole zombie thing? Yeah, technically creating zombies or using necromancy was forbidden. Mom took creative liberties with the law all the time, and since the last inspector who'd come along had mysteriously turned into a statue of butter, the city board pretended not to notice.

"Uh, got a little constipated, Mom."

I made the obligatory grunting sounds and glared at the other three to keep them quiet. Natasha warned me mentally about how lying was a sin.

"I have some stool softeners," Mom said. "Want me to bring you some?"

"No, I'm okay."

I glared at Greg, who was snickering into his hands.

"Are you sure? Wait right there, Boris. I have just the thing. Sentient laxative pills!"

Crap.

I heard her high heels clicking down the hall, and looked desperately at my arm. It was red and swollen and the hex mark was still there. I grabbed all the different soaps—from lilac scented to the specialty stuff used to get zombie goo stains out of the rugs—and started smearing everyone single one on my arm and scrubbing it with a washcloth.

I'd either have the cleanest hex mark in all of history at this rate, or no skin left on my arm around it. Nothing was working.

Greg collapsed on the floor, kicking his hooves and hooting with laughter. Doomkitty gave him a disdainful look and licked a paw. Natasha swam pensively in the soapy sink.

"What is so funny?" I snapped.

Greg lost it. He howled with laugher and pounded his fists and hooves on the tiles. I swear if he could have turned any brighter red, he would be glowing. "You... can't... wash... the Mark... off! Ahahahahahaha!"

I stared. "What?"

He started wiping smoking tears from his eyes, cackling. "Only a Magi Superior can get it off." He doubled over, straining to breathe. "Washing it off... oh, brimstones below... that's priceless..."

I sat down hard. It wasn't washable ink? Or the mark itself was too powerful that it'd manifested into something else once drawn? I didn't know any Magi Superiors! They were all in Washington.

Well, except for the headmaster at school, but he'd tried to feed me to the Leviathan. He wasn't going to *help* me now.

Mom knocked on the door again. "Boris, honey, I found those pills for you."

8.

Mom slipped a small plastic container under the door with a quick modification of the door atoms.

Three blue and pink capsules leapt out of the container and charged me, bellowing about the loosening of stool.

I jumped away as they started climbing my shoe. I stomped on them, but they dodged and kept coming, aiming for my mouth. I shook my leg frantically and grabbed the door handle.

"Are they working, dear?"

I swatted at the capsules and they squirmed out of my hands and dove for my face. I backpedaled, tripped over the claw-footed bathtub, and landed hard on my butt inside. I clenched my teeth as the capsules pulled at my lips and tried to force their way into my mouth.

"Mmmph!"

Wildly, I looked for a weapon to destroy them with, and spotted the toilet. I scrambled out of the tub and crawled across to it, then flipped up the seat and thought as hard as I could at the pills about how many enemies were in the sewage system. Squeezing my eyes shut, I dunked my head in the toilet bowl.

With bubbling gurgles of delight and proclamations of the inevitable defeat of all waste, the pills torpedoed down the flusher. I jerked back, gasping and sputtering and wiping my mouth. Ugh.

"Boris?"

I looked around. I needed to get out of here.

The window by the sink was still there, though now it was a hexagonal shape with lacy curtains and didn't have a crank to open it with. I waved for everyone to be quiet and peeked out. It was three stories down. I didn't care to try my levitation or gravity neutralizer spells again.

"Mrow?" Doomkitty head-butted my knee. I moved aside. Doomkitty sat, licked a paw, and then casually pressed that paw against the window and pushed.

The window exploded outward, taking a huge section of the wall with it. I gaped. So did Greg.

The house groaned and started to repair the structural damage, smoothing over the ragged two-by-fours and siding with a glossy coating of slime that would reform into a new window soon.

Doomkitty stretched and flexed all its wings.

"Boris! Do you need more pills? That sounded pretty bad, honey."

"I'm okay, Mom, really."

I jumped on Doomkitty's back. What the heck, the worst that could happen was we all fell and the lion cushioned the landing, right?

Doomkitty swelled its chest and roared. I saw blue sparks and golden thrones and a wash of vertigo pounded over me in a mob-like stampede for Black Friday broom accessory deals. Greg wailed.

"My God, Boris! Don't worry, sweetheart, I'm coming to the rescue!"

"Fly," I said as the door started creaking with atomic manipulation. I reached back and grabbed Greg by the arm just before Doomkitty launched itself into empty space.

It was Greg who was screaming (not me) as we plummeted three stories down, a brick load on a feather. We were going to splat on the rosebushes below. Since they were carnivorous mutations designed to apprehend and eat burglars, I didn't think we'd last too long once we hit the ground.

Then Doomkitty started flapping its wings. I muttered prayers for every pantheon I could think of and squeezed my eyes shut, clutching Doomkitty's mane. Greg babbled in Hellion.

Why there was this totally sucky urge to *look* at the rosebushes, I had no freaking idea. But Doomkitty wasn't gaining any altitude and the roses hissed and clicked their teeth.

So I peeked. We were hovering about halfway down from the window and above the garden. Doomkitty pumped its wings, panting.

"We're not dead," I said.

We dropped about three feet and one of the taller bushes snaked up and almost caught Doomkitty's tail.

"Never mind! Go forward, dude, go forward!" I leaned in that direction, and felt Greg lean into me too.

"It's a bit hard to do that when your house shields are holding me back," Doomkitty said irritably.

"You talk?"

"Shocking, I know. Do you want to lend some assistance here? And by the way, I am not a dude."

There were so many gender options to choose from, so I took a wild guess. "You're a girl?"

"Naturally."

Score! "Got it," I said aloud.

I twisted around and looked behind us. Mom hung out of the opening.

"Boris Tchaikovsky Göttenal," Mom said in her you-are-so-in-trouble-now-young-man voice. She had the house shield leash wrapped around one hand and the fluctuating cords of power were twisted around Doomkitty's hind legs. "*What* did you do to my bathroom window?"

"Can't talk now, Mom. I'm, uh, late for after curricular, um... revolutionary theoretic study. I get extra credit and I can count it towards a college degree."

She beamed, all the anger melting away. "Boris, why didn't you tell me? I thought about taking that course when I was in school." She leaned her elbows on the opening ledge and looked dreamily out into space. "You know, if I hadn't met that Dr. Cortestfield and been inspired in the reanimation of dead tissue in junior year..."

Doomkitty growled and two wings sagged. We lurched closer to the roses.

"Um, Mom, can this wait?"

"...it was her smile and the way she brought that dead opera singer back to life and had her sing an aria to me..."

Frantic, I looked down. A rose bud was drooling at me.

Okay. I focused on the end of the house-shield leash Mom held and quietly stole it from her. She rambled on about how hot Dr. Cortestfield was.

I sneaked the leash away and snapped it. Doomkitty lurched forward and did a complete three-hundred-sixty-degree flip. I almost lost my lunch *again*. The roses snapped and hissed at us, stretching out thorny stems.

"Fly like hell and get us out of here!" I yelled at Doomkitty.

"Wrong alignment," Greg and Doomkitty said in unison.

Doomkitty lurched away from the house and then crash-landed in the yard. I went flying head over heels off and crashed into something bulky, solid, and unmoving.

I bounced off and landed hard on my butt. I'm fairly sure it's not scientifically possible to turn white as a sheet without face paint, but I'm not a scientist and that's what it *felt* like. I'd found out what had set off the trespasser alarms.

9.

It was a web troll.

And if you're thinking of internet trolls, or trolls that live under bridges, or those little plastic dolls with neon hair my dad thinks are cute, um, no. Web trolls are made out of webs.

This one was ten feet tall, sticky white like a badly wrapped mummy, sort of humanoid in shape, with bulges along its arms that might have been muscles, or something else. I didn't like to think what. Because, really, it had those weird bulges all over. A huge pair of spider mandibles jutted out of its lumpy head, and it had lots of multi-faceted eyes, and a stinger poking out of its butt.

It was slurping down one of the zombies, and lumbering stickily towards the house. And me. Since, you know, I was between it and the house.

Greg babbled in Babylonian and Doomkitty squeaked.

"Shut up," I hissed, an octave higher than usual.

The web troll turned its eight red eyes towards us and finished slurping down the zombie. The former corpse's gray toes wiggled as it was swallowed and a new lump created a bas-relief on the troll's stomach.

If we made any sudden moves, it'd shoot us with webs and make *us* its next meal. According to my first year field guide, the only existing web trolls were *supposed* to be in the San Francisco Zoo. I should have paid attention to the news more.

"We should run like hell," Greg whispered.

I would have agreed if not for the fact the troll was less than ten feet away and its web-spitting could reach twice that.

The troll took another step towards us, its mouth mandibles clicking. That's when I noticed it wore a radio collar that was glowing with a puppet spell. We weren't allowed to learn puppet spells after the incident of the puppet teacher parade twenty years ago. It'd become a regular urban legend.

The collar glowed snot-green and had flecks of purple like rotten grapes in it. Someone had broken the troll out of the zoo—all the way in San Francisco—and warped it over here to *my* yard? That didn't make any sense why *I'd* be the one picked on. No one knew I'd swiped the spell from the archives before we left.

Well. Except—

The troll scraped some of its webby skin into its hands and stuffed the wad in its mouth and started to chew. Ugh, and I thought the zombies chewing off their thumbs was gross.

The troll snorted, hawked, and spat the web at us with full force.

I dove to the side with incredible speed. I might try out for track and field next year. I heard Greg shrieking in some dead language, but I was too busy taking his advice and running like hell.

Then Doomkitty yowled. "Help! Boris!"

Purple lightning flickered overhead frequently enough to give me light to see by, and despite knowing that in *every horror movie ever made* if you looked over your shoulder while running, you'd trip and fall and get eaten... Well. I looked. I know. I suck.

I spun around. Greg was hightailing it across the lawn and vaulted the wooden fence behind the garage. The web had missed him and me, but it'd trapped Doomkitty in a sticky white mess on the grass.

Great.

The troll loomed over Doomkitty and reached down with huge claws. I didn't think Doomkitty would pop out of its stomach *Alien*-style like Natasha did.

But I couldn't fight a web troll!

I ran towards the troll anyway.

Doomkitty thrashed as much as being webified to the grass let you thrash, which wasn't much. The troll leaned down, mandibles wide.

"Step away from the holy cat!" I waved my arms in a bad case of heroic distractionism. "Yeah, you, spider-butt!"

The troll turned, still bent over, and thrust its head towards me, chewing another wad of web. I hurled myself to one side as the web came flying at me. It splatted just behind me. I landed on my hands and knees and scrambled up, dodging like a drunken squirrel on the highway.

I felt sticky, gooey nastiness thwip around my ankles and I landed hard on my face. Ow. I kicked and struggled, but my feet were webbed down. I knew exactly how The Fly felt in the end of the original movie.

I sorta flopped over onto my back and frantically searched for a de-webbing or de-trapping spell. The troll lurched with sticky steps toward me, leaving residual webbing on the grass.

"*Untrapinitius*," I muttered. "*Dewebifius*? Blast it, *unstick*!"

It wasn't working.

The troll loomed over me and it smelled like zombie farts and squashed spiders. I gagged. One huge, white, cobwebby hand reached for my face.

"Flame on!" I panicked and set the web troll on fire.

The grimoire thrummed, I felt a rush of power and smelled brimstone, and suddenly the troll was burning gloriously as the webs fried. I flung my arm across my face.

The web troll bellowed and toppled over in a massive bonfire. The heat seared my face worse than sunburn and I scooted away as fast as I could.

Greg popped up behind my shoulder and cackled. He patted me on the back as plumes of black and red smoke polluted the air. Right now, I didn't care about the carbon footprint that would leave.

"You're tapping into the Pit already, kid," Greg said. "That means you've got less than an hour left and already you're turning to the dark side. We'll make a proper Beast minion out of you yet."

Oh, crap, what had I just done?

10.

I stared at Greg, feeling like I'd eaten too many s'mores too fast and then drank a two liter of Pepsi. My stomach hurt and I wanted to puke. There was a running theme in my day. "An hour?"

"Sure," Greg said cheerfully. "You wonder why that troll got sicced on you by your headmaster? Because you're this close to ending the world, kid! Congratulations."

"Wait! How do you know the headmaster sent the troll?"

Greg opened his mouth, closed it, danced around in a circle while cursing, then sulkily looked at me. He held up my iPod. Yeah, again.

"I was trying to get Lite FM," Greg said, "and got the spell-radio control signals instead. A time-temporal rift planted the troll in his office half an hour ago so he decided to use it."

"Give me that." I snatched the iPod, made mental gagging sounds as I popped in the ear buds—I didn't even want to think about it—and sure enough, I heard the command spell hijacking the radio waves.

Destroy Boris Göttenal. Destroy Boris Göttenal. Destroy...

So. I had a hex on my arm, the Most Forbidden Grimoire Ever attached to my chest, I'd started a hexpocolypse, I'd acquired an imp from Hell and a heavenly furball, and now the headmaster at school was aiming for new lows. He wouldn't just flunk me, or expel me—he wanted me dead. Again!

The half-million dollar question was what the living heck did I do now?

"So what the living heck do we do now?" I asked, when no one was cool enough to volunteer a perfect solution on the spot.

I felt like there was a giant alarm clock hanging over my head, like that Greek dude in the myth. Only he had some steak knife or a sword or whatever hanging by a string over his head. I bet OSHA had regulations against that. Or WOSHA, the warlock/witch sister agency.

When the troll had gone up in flames like a marshmallow over a campfire, the webs had disintegrated off Doomkitty. She sat up and now was grooming herself as if nothing had happened.

Greg stuffed his hands in his pockets and whistled, looking innocent.

"Argh," I said. "Both of you are useless."

I counted off what I had. A double-crossing imp who snitched my stuff. Doomkitty. The grimoire.

Pause, rewind. The grimoire.

I was holding the most forbidden, powerful spell book in the known world. Or, well, at least in the state.

If I could find a spell to stop the headmaster turning me into a gooey stain on the road, wall, or bathroom floor, and get him to remove the hex, I could fix all this. And I might not even get expelled.

"Grimoire," I said politely. "I need to read you for a spell to fix this mess."

It sighed but unstuck and I flipped it open.

"Don't you think it might be more productive to do that on the way?" Doomkitty asked. "We're down to fifty-five minutes."

"Fifty-four," Greg said, and cackled.

I glared at him, and climbed on Doomkitty's back. Greg rode behind me, and we launched into the air. My stomach got left behind, but baggage shipped it ahead and it caught up once we were flapping over the street, or what was left of it after an angel crater.

"So why *are* dead angels falling, Greg?"

"Heart attacks," the imp said. "Or strokes. I forget. Anyway, they weren't ready for the apocalypse to start now, so they freaked out."

"Oh."

I focused on the grimoire after that. Most of the pages were encrypted but the pictures were creepy enough I decided most of them probably weren't a good old fashioned persuasion spell. Unless you wanted your mind ripped out and replaced with radio circuits or onions instead.

"C'mon," I said as Doomkitty swooped at warp ten through the suburbs and we came in sight of the school.

I was planning to face the headmaster. The guy had tried to kill me! And what was I going to do? Walk up to him and say, "Yo, teach, can we discuss this civilly and end the threat to the end of the world?"

He'd be so, "Right on, bro, let's settle this peaceful like." And make a truce sign or something.

Actually, he'd probably blast me on sight. So I needed a way to sneak up on him first.

"Oh, man, we're so screwed," I muttered, and kept tuning pages.

The grimoire suggested something that would leave the headmaster in a gooey puddle. A gooey puddle on the floor that *talked*. The snarky magic carpet Jake Horner and I had done for the experiment fair was still fresh in my mind, and I always cringed a bit walking on rugs afterwards. I'd had to get my pinky surgically grafted on again after SnarkRug had turned PyschoRug.

"No," I said to the book. "I was hoping something, um, a little less violent."

It suggested one that would turn him into stone, ice, wood, clay, tofu, and maple syrup.

"How about something that doesn't transmogrify him?"

The grimoire offered the Spell of Smiting (just what it sounded like), the Incarcerator (imprisoned forever in a soap dish), and the Terminator Redux (sent somewhere else in time—probably as a cyborg).

I yelled as Doomkitty did a barrel roll and dropped to the baseball diamond behind the east wing of the school.

My legs were giving jelly a run for its money and I slid off the lion's back.

Greg and Doomkitty watched me. It occurred to me Doomkitty was almost full grown, and she'd been getting bigger every minute since I'd first seen her.

"You're not coming?" I asked.

"Conflict of interests," Greg said.

Doomkitty avoided my wounded and betrayed gaze. "I'll watch your back. From out here."

"You mean you expect me to go in there alone?" My voice did interesting things several octaves higher than normal. "By myself?"

Doomkitty's tail twitched. Greg studied his claws.

"Better get going," Greg said, when I still stood there in horror.

Even the grimoire abandoned me at that point. It clearly had no spells I could use, and thudded to the ground. I couldn't pick it up—it had either glued itself there or weighed eight thousand tons.

I glanced back at the school. "How do we know he's even in there?"

"That's where the signal was broadcast from," Greg said. "Besides. He's faculty. Where else would he be?"

Right. And he was probably waiting for me.

I needed a plan, but I didn't have one.

I needed some spells, but I couldn't think of any.

I needed to get the heck out of there. Instead, I started creeping towards the building and the ultimate showdown.

It occurred to me just then that I had been wearing a red shirt all day.

11.

Inside, the school was warped into flashing emergency lights and empty halls. You only saw it this empty on spring break, after you got trampled by everyone else heading for the doors.

I kind of had that same dazed, achy feeling when I peeked around the side entrance doorframe. It was quiet here. I mean, dangerously-ominously-something-bad's-about-to-happen-to-you kind of quiet.

My tennis shoe squeaked and I winced at each squelch-squish. I didn't even want to know what I'd stepped in to get it squeaky. And I'd forgotten to change, so I only had one. My other sock was sticky.

Okay, so if the headmaster was theoretically still in the building, that meant he'd be in his office. The Office.

I swallowed hard.

I kicked off my shoe, peeled off my sweaty socks and tiptoed barefoot through the hallway towards the headmaster's office.

My brain was screaming at me how absolutely fricking stupid I was being, exclamation point, exclamation point. I didn't argue with it. If I wasn't so freaked out about being spotted and toasted by a death ray, I would have been screaming myself

Up ahead, I spied the door to the headmaster's office. It was ajar, and a steady chanting came from inside. Usually any ritual chanting, plus end of the world in the near future, plus the possibility of the one responsible being within a hundred mile radius, equaled some really nasty spell.

The school wasn't allowed to keep hair and blood samples with records, especially after the scandal of the newt eyes back in my dad's high school days. But that didn't necessarily mean the headmaster, being uber-powerful and practically omnipotent—or is it omnipresent? Omniscient? Over-easy?—couldn't rig something up to blast me into oblivion.

I didn't really think Natasha's God was on speaking terms with me after this mess up, so I stuck to hoping as hard as I could that I would figure something out. The ticking clock wasn't helping.

I'll eat all my vegetables, I started thinking, and feed the zombies, and not flush Natasha down the toilet again, and I swear I'll do anything else, just please, please, please—

I could hear the words now. It was Old Spelivan and Latin and something else, something guttural that made you want to gag mentally, and while I didn't understand it, I didn't think I should let him finish. You know, in case I ended up dead.

So I peeked around the door. The headmaster sat in a protective circle and he was summoning something that looked like the Creature from the Black Lagoon's worst nightmare. It had these tufts of shadow sticking out of its head and it had Badass with a capital B practically stamped on it.

Necromancy was illegal. Summoning demons could get you a life sentence.

But creating a shadow self, a shadsel, was, like, the sin of all sins.

You had to almost twist your very existence inside out and it sucked a lot of power and life and karma from all around you. We were taught about it in the Top Ten Things You Never Do, Or You're In Such Trouble You'd Be Better Off Not Existing, Because We Will Hunt You Down and Destroy You, which was a PowerPoint presentation at the beginning of every semester. Or more frequently if necessary.

It was really, *really*, REALLY Bad.

I suddenly did not want to be there.

"Dude," I squeaked.

The headmaster looked up, and I suddenly I had an all new definition of the evil eye.

Oh, crap.

"Wait!" I screamed. "I can fix this if you just erase the hex!"

He didn't stop his incantations.

I tried to run, but suddenly his office wards snapped around me and rooted me in place. My eyes almost bulged out of my head. I could give any bug a run for its money. Bring it on.

"Killing me won't stop this," I said. I hoped that was true, anyway. "All I need is a reversal spell on the hex in the next, um, five minutes, and everything will be solved. Just think of your record! Do dead students really look good on transcripts and résumés?"

Oh. Wait, he didn't *need* those. And no one would know, aside from my Mom.

I squirmed and got spectacularly nowhere. I looked around for something to steal and break free. Unlike in the movies, I didn't have enough muscle mass to get mad and burst free with a basso roar.

"Sir, I swear, I'll never try to end the world again! Please just pause this and think about it a minute! Don't make this mistake—cancel—"

He raised his hands for the final gesture and I sensed him ready to speak the final words.

The shadsel writhed and reached for me from the confining circle within the protective ring. It opened its mouth and showed shiny black teeth that were long and pointy and dripping poisonous venom or something worse.

This is for your own good, and the world at large, the headmaster projected at me. The other attempts did not work, and I won't use spells that can be traced back to me. Good bye, Mr. Göttenal. Kindly stay dead this time.

I gasped. It wasn't the noblest of death speeches, but I couldn't quite manage a shriek.

"Endutus summonucus..." he said.

I squeezed my eyes shut and did the only thing I could think of: I stole the words right out of his mouth.

12.

The words were sticky and tingly in my hands, and since I was clenching my fists so tight to begin with, the words got mushed up into a sweaty ball and garbled.

Silence followed. I didn't get blasted into an unrecognizable stain the on the floor.

He looked blankly at me, his mouth hanging open. The shadsel writhed in its cage, but with the spell broken it dissolved. The headmaster's body collapsed and the circles broke around him. The wards cracked.

I fell on my back.

The headmaster was out cold.

I staggered up, crawled over, and shook him like I did Natasha when she wouldn't shut up at night. "C'mon, man, *wake up* or the world's gonna *end*!"

He looked drained worse than a zombie snack. But he was still breathing, just passed out cold. I was about to go into shock.

Soap and water and something as powerful as the headmaster washing off the hex...

I sprinted out the door, down the hall, and skidded into the boys' bathroom. "Greg!" I screamed. "Get your fiery red butt in here right now!"

He popped out of the urinal. I wasn't asking.

"What's up? We've got a minute left."

"Does the headmaster have to be awake and conscious and making an effort to remove the hex?" I soaked a handful of paper towels, lathered them in soap, and ran back to the office.

Greg tailed me, and Doomkitty came racing down the hall.

Scaredy cat.

"Dunno," Greg said, picking his nose. He tried wiping his finger on my dripping paper towels and I yanked them away.

"Answer me truthfully." I glared at him. "Does he or does he not have to be awake and cooperating?"

Greg sulked and perched on the edge of the desk. He started juggling paperweights. "Yep."

I looked at Doomkitty. "Wake him up."

The winged lion raised an eyebrow, Spock-like. No, I swear, she really did!

"How?"

"Bite him!" I screamed. "How should I know? The world is ending in thirty seconds, you useless holy furball!"

Doomkitty fluttered her wings, and gave the headmaster a big juicy lick across the face. He started and sputtered.

I shoved the paper towels into his hand, forced his now soapy grip towards my arm, and lied like crazy. "Sir, quick, someone's just written down the Endocrinal Code on your favorite faculty mug, and you need to spell and wipe it off."

"Wha...?" He squinted, but his grip tightened on the towels.

"Quick," I said. "Use a cleansing spell and wipe it off or it'll be permanent."

"Mr. Göttenal…"

"Do it," Doomkitty said, looming over him. "Or I'll eat you."

Greg started a countdown. "Ten! Nine!"

Dazedly, the headmaster rubbed at my arm.

"Eight! Seven!"

I bit my lip, about to explode. Maybe literally, who knew.

Nothing happened.

"Six! Five!"

"Power, dude," I reminded him. "Use the force. Um. Magic."

Something stabbed my arm. Hot pain wrapped around my bicep and the hex writhed and started to fade, peeling off my skin and leaving a huge red blister. I yelped.

"Four, three, two!"

The hex fell to the floor and I stomped on it. "Be gone, sucker!"

"One—"

A puff of hieroglyphic smoke curled around my foot and then the world went black.

For two seconds. It was just the power shorting out and then the generators kicking back on.

I peeked down at my arm. Aside from a nasty burn, the hex was gone. The headmaster was groaning and footsteps echoed in the hall.

"Damn it!" Greg did a small dance of rage. "Now I'm going to go back to kitchen duty..."

"Byeeeee," I told him, and he vanished in a blink of red light.

Doomkitty went invisible. "I'll be around."

Where was *that* trick when we could have used it?

I nodded, in that state between laughing and fainting.

Then it was just me and the headmaster in his office, until the dean poked her head in.

"Boris? Mark?" The dean squinted. "What's going on?"

"Well, the hexpocolypse is on hold again for now," I said.

Then I promptly blacked out.

13.

I got a few days off and the world went back to normal. Mom was still clueless and Zoe was reversed into girl form again. She moped about not being a plant-hybrid. Mom told her she could transform on her own once she was older.

I hadn't seen Greg since the Office, but the little twerp took my iPod back to Hell with him. However, Doomkitty had shown up in my bedroom, and said that she'd stick around for a bit. I'd always wanted a pet winged lion with lots of eyes from Revelations.

Of course Natasha didn't shut up for two days straight so I flushed her down the toilet just out of spite. I bet she made war with those sentient laxative pills before she showed up again in a bottle of Mountain Dew.

I swore off soda for awhile.

The angel craters were slowly repaired with taxpayer dollars, all the apocalyptic things were sucked back into whatever pits they had come from, and except for the holes in streets and buildings and the fact that lots of the doomsayers who'd finally gotten their heyday were out of work again, the world was repaired pretty well.

We ended up getting a new headmaster after ours retired the day after I stuffed the hexpocolypse back into the prophecy pipeline and things started normalizing. She was some former professor over at Warlock & Yale. She was *really* old, like ancient. In her forties at least. She wore yellow-tinted shades, and a baggy Hawaiian shirt and Bermuda shorts all the time.

But at least she didn't expel me. She started lecturing me in her office, got distracted by the stock market hike, and just told me not to do that "ending the world prematurely" stuff again. I made record time getting out of the office.

After last period, as I packed up my books, I saw Steven and the other guys by their lockers.

One thing was for sure, facing down monsters and teachers and sentient laxative pills had done quite a bit for my backbone growth. Sure, I still looked like the wimpy class geek, but I had to make sure Steven and his buddies—whom I most definitely did *not* want to be friends with now—wouldn't try this stunt again.

"Hey, Steve, dude." I waved and walked over. Actually, I strutted—until I tripped over my shoelaces and almost did a nosedive into the floor.

The guys grinned and ringed me in.

"Heya, Boris," Steven said. "I got a little job for you."

"First things first, Steve-o," I said.

The others exchanged smirky glances. Ha ha, look at Boris trying to stand up to the coolest kid. What a riot!

I punched Steven in the nose.

"That's for the hex." I smacked him again, just because he was gaping at me in shock, like he couldn't believe I'd punched him. I was still processing that too. "And that's for being a jerk. I'm not going to steal anything more for you, and if you ever try putting more hexes on me, man, I'll sic a three-hundred-pound winged lion on you."

Doomkitty prowled around the corner of the hall, mostly invisible except to Steven and the guys. They did hilarious ghost impersonations and fled.

I grinned and leaned an elbow against Doomkitty's shoulder. Life was mostly back to normal and I'd learned a valuable lesson. What it was, I wasn't sure, but I'd learned it.

"I don't think they'll be trouble anymore."

Doomkitty purred. "If they really must go put hexes on something, they should do it on themselves. After all…"

I groaned. "Don't even say it—"

Doomkitty looked smug. "Hex always marks the spot."

Steadyboi After the Apocalypse

You trudge through another wasteland town, sticking to the narrow roads, trying not to make the potholes deeper or the dust clouds thicker, but it's hard when you're a hulking robot built for a war long gone. You sheared off your guns and dislocated your laser fuses, dumped your ammo stores in a bog, and snapped the various killing blades into nubs[1].

People don't believe your painted chassis.

You spend a lot of your energy gleaned from solar panels on scrubbing mud and rust off so the English letters are legible. You don't have a way to speak, and when you gesture with your blocky hands (made to crush and punch and smash)

[1] CN: war aftermath, gun violence, lung disease, sickness, death

people think you're violent. So you grind your slow, plodding way deeper into the wastes. You can't help going through towns: your core programming guidance system overrules any detours. You were made to confront people, even if you don't want to cause harm.

You're a huge, heavy, metal monster. And since there aren't any wars, you're obsolete. You'd offer to let people take you apart—re-use your heat core (or your innards or your rivets or your exoskeleton or your optics or your pistons or your thick, steel-plated skin or your targeting system or your intelligence cortex) if it'd help make their lives easier—but everyone is too scared. People think you'll self-destruct if captured. You won't, because you fried that system feature once you got away from the army. You never saw combat so you want to be useful.

The world is trying to rebuild. You could help, but none of the people will let you.

Onward you trudge. Reports are that far, far into the northern ash plains, there are pits so deep that even a robot like you couldn't climb out. The floods will wash silt and mud and char into the recesses, and you'll shut down without any sunlight, and then no one has to be afraid.

(You're not sure if you can be afraid for yourself yet. That's categorized under self-defense protocols, and you also disabled those once you left the base. You don't want to hurt anyone, not the way the makers intended.)

This town is just like the others: battered by heat-storms, half-empty from the plagues, straining to hold onto a shape and a purpose and a name. You grind your way down the only street wide enough for a twelve-foot, three-ton hulking war machine.

Your optics register infrared heat signatures in buildings and hidden behind rusted cars and barricaded junk. Population: seventy-five. You hesitate by a single stop light, all the glass shattered and the wire sagging in the middle. There's a pair of leather shoes dangling next to the acid-crusted shell. It's probably too high up for the civilians to access.

Carefully, you extend one hand and pluck the shoes between jointed fingers. You lay them down at the side of the road. Someone should be able to use the leather.

And someone does. An adolescent-model human stands on the sidewalk, staring at you. You look back. Their chassis is covered by a floral-pattern dress. They are barefoot and hold a cloth toy in skinny arms. Their hair follicles are curly and black, swept into a round helmet-like structure. Analysis: child, malnourished, unafraid, sad.

"You better get outta here," the small human says. "Pa ain't much fond of warbots."

You cautiously point at your chest plate, where you scrubbed away the dirt so the letters are visible. The paint is chipping and you don't have any resources to re-apply a chemical sealant.

NOT A THREAT
WANT PEACE
PLZ NO HARM

The small human shakes their head. The larger adult humans remain hidden from visual analysis.

You lower your arm, defeated, and take a step past the streetlight.

"Hey, wait!"

The small human has put the shoes on their feet, increasing their environmental protection status by several degrees, which you approve of. They run up to you, their fabric toy—analysis: lupine design, denim structure, cotton-filled; a wolf plushie—gripped in one hand. In the other hand, the small human holds up a singular piece of paper.

"It's a sticker," they say, peeling off the self-adhesive shape. "Was gonna save it but I reckon you need it more. Thanks muchly for my shoes back."

The small human gestures for you to extend your hand. Cautiously, you lower your arm and offer the back of your blocky fist. The child presses the sticker against your metal and pats it. You examine the design: a humanoid exoskeleton painted red and gold, suspended in white clouds.

"It's Iron Man," the child says. "Pa says he was a good guy."

Then an adult-model voice bellows from inside a store: "Rhiannon! Get away from that thing now!"

"Bye," the small human says, and dashes away.

The adult-model catches them by an arm and yanks them inside the building. The infrared signals retreat.

You activate the movement for wave-non-lethal.exe in your memory banks and flex your fingers in an awkward claw.

No other people come out of hiding.

You rumble onwards, leaving town. Once you're at the end of the last street, you rotate your wrist joint so the back of your hand faces your chassis. Easier to see the sticker and keep it safe from the weather that way.

There are no more Rhiannons in the towns you pass through, so you protect your Iron Man sticker as long as you can. It lasts a month before it peels away in a dust storm and you can't catch it.

You walk into a gully that used to be a subway in a city that used to exist. No infrared signals anywhere for miles. Dry weeds and scrawny trees strain from the rubble. Radiation levels are still in the red for human survival. Your metal frame is designed to absorb the heat and repel the rads, so you don't have to stop or detour this place.

You've got to be close to the ash plain pits. Maps loaded into your memory banks indicate that the terrain was devastated by nuclear backlash from the ruptured missile silos. Too bad your odometer was scrambled when you deactivated your targeting system. It's hard to track milage by sight alone.

Still, your destination must be close. You've been traveling for thirteen weeks, six days, four hours and twenty-three minutes. Your average speed is five miles per hour in clear weather.

A signal hits your FM radio.

"This is restricted territory! No bots! Screw off!"

You hesitate. The high ruins of old cement architecture create a one-way path, and it has narrowed to a point difficult for you to pivot and retreat.

You send a short-wave radio burst with a pre-fabricated message.

<NON-HOSTILE ON APPROACH. DO NOT ENGAGE. NON-HOSTILE SEEKS PASSAGE FOR PEACEFUL TRAVEL. VIOLENCE IS NOT REQUIRED.>

"Declare your armament specs!"

<NON-FUNCTIONAL.>

There is a fifteen second delay.

"Okay, come in, slagbot."

Cheered by the invitation, you plod forward. The tunnel opens up into a wide open space piled with heaps of scrap.

"Stop on the X and hold still."

The sign is a ten meter pair of red-painted lines at an intersection of cleared cement. You stop as directed. A half dozen heat signatures pop up from shielding around the area.

Live humans are good. You wait for further instructions.

A hum of machinery alarms you, and a pair of turrets rise from behind a lead-plated wall.

You recognize the cannon barrels. Old G-X77 models, designed for taking out long-range missiles and aircraft. If it's loaded with war-grade explosive heads, a single shot will rip you apart.

This isn't how you wanted to deactivate. It's so violent. You don't want to be a war machine. You realize how much you don't want to be blown apart like one, either.

You raise your hands in the surrender-pose.exe.

<PLEASE DO NOT ATTACK. NON-HOSTILE WILL LEAVE PEACEFULLY.>

A pair of adult-model humans wave EMP rifles from nearby the cannons. Their voices are high and register fear and hostility.

"Shoot it! Shoot it before it kills the rest of us!"

The cannons heat up. You don't have enough shielding to deflect a shot this close, and you were built as a tank unit; you can't easily dodge.

You deactivate your optics and mute your infrared scanner. It's not going to stop you getting blown into scrap. It somehow hurts less when you don't see it coming, though.

When you first came online, the world was already over. Nuclear spring clashed with the catastrophic climate degradation.

Your non-maker technician communicated with you via short-wave frequencies and text-based transmissions. Their name was Alicia McReedy. They called you Steadyboi. That was not an official designation for your make and model. You didn't mind, though. You liked having a name.

"I've been making some adjustments," Alicia McReedy told you. Sometimes they broadcasted through direct audio interface links so you heard their voice. This method was less efficient, since their vocalizations were often interrupted by ongoing respiratory failure. A cough, they said, and texted: *I'll be fine.*

"It's not really free will in the sense philosophers argue about," Alicia McReedy said. "But what do they know? We're just meat programmed with electric currents and anxiety."

A cough, louder than before.

"Okay, so listen, Steadyboi. I'm overriding your obedience matrix and uploading a bunch of pacifist and community-support protocols which you can self-apply once reviewed. You're the last one off the assembly line, buddy. Wish this had ended different for all of us, you know? Hell, I'm the last human standing in this place, too."

They sighed.

"I'm not giving you orders. No point, heh. No war left to fight. Besides, I'm a scientist, not a soldier. Runs in my family. My daughter and husband were in different fields and... I'm gonna cry if I try to talk about them. Even with Kendra's notes, it's too late for me. I don't honestly know if there's anyone alive who can benefit from her findings, you know? I'm so proud of her."

A long interruption, heightened with distress.

"So here's the deal, pal. You go out there and you find yourself a purpose, okay? I'm giving you resources, and I'm hoping there's someone left somewhere who'll want to help you. Or you them. I don't know."

A heavy coughing fit.

Alicia McReedy switched to text input.

I may have lied about being fine. Sorry, buddy. But look. There's nothing you can do for me; my lungs are shot, and all I can do for you is let you go and hope you'll be okay out there. You're a good bot, Steadyboi. Just remember you can choose who you are. All people do. Good luck. See you on the flip side, huh?

And then no more communications came from Alicia McReedy, though you waited and waited and waited.

You experience what your logs refer to as *surprise* when you come online again.

Infrared scans indicate three heat signatures. You activate your optics and scan your surroundings. An adult-model, an adolescent-model, and a canine-model quadruped known as a "dog."

The smaller human is asleep against the dog's side in one corner of the warehouse. Both their heart rates are steady.

"Hey, warbot. Remember me?"

Your optics scan the adult-model human. Their vocal register is deeper and their body has grown and widened. It is Rhiannon, who gave you the Iron Man sticker. Time must have passed; humans, you've learned, do not upgrade very fast.

You nod, neck joints grinding. Every part of you is stiff. Ball joints are rusted and your entire left arm is non-functional. The hydraulics in your legs are crusted in dirt. Even with all the damage from neglect and weather, you're operational. You're alive.

Rhiannon grins. "Been awhile. Steadyboi, right? I've been working on digging you out from the scrap heap. Thought I recognized your rig." They pat your half-curled hand, right where the sticker used to go.

Tentatively, you ping Rhiannon with a short-burst message. <YOU FIXED NON-HOSTILE STEADYBOI?>

They twitch one shoulder, glancing at a thin tablet strapped to their wrist. "Kinda. It's hard finding parts that work with your build."

<NON-HOSTILE THANKS HUMAN.>

"Don't thank me yet," Rhiannon says. They grunt as they reach down and pick up a tool belt slotted with a mechanic's equipment. "I don't think you'll ever be a top-notch warbot again. Those weapon mods? Fried beyond saving."

<STEADYBOI IS NON-HOSTILE. DO NO HARM. PEACEFUL.>

"Wait... you wrecked your guns yourself?"

<AFFIRMATIVE.>

They cough. It makes them sound like Alicia McReedy and you have a concern. Are they going to malfunction too?

<HUMAN IN NEED OF REPAIR?>

Rhiannon waves a gloved hand. It looks like emotion-dismissive.exe, which one of Alicia

McReedy's assistants used often. "Don't we all. I'll be fine, Steadyboi."

Internal alarms whir in your processors. Alicia McReedy was not fine. They shut down. You do not want Rhiannon to shut down.

They look up at you, frowning. "What's the matter with you? Never heard of dust-lung before?"

<HUMAN IS IN NEED OF REPAIR.>

Rhiannon sighs, which leads to more coughing. "Yeah, yeah. You know, as a kid, I wished I was a bot. Felt like it'd be so much easier to just swap out some parts and get on with living, you know? But humans are just mush with a few bonier bits holding them together. We don't even get exoskeletons." They kick a rusted bucket, which collapses under their boot in a puff of dried flakes. "I'm not Iron Man."

You run a search through your downloaded memory logs; you have the database nodes Alicia McReedy installed, though you have had no reason to index them before. All the information was tagged as biological-medical-enhancement.

There are no results for "Iron Man."

"Look, you're low on ion cells," Rhiannon says. "And I don't want you clunking around and waking up my brother or Todd." They gesture at the smaller human and the dog-model. Both are now snoring. "Go into power-save mode. I've got some solar-panels to rig you with so you can recharge on your own when the sun comes back up. I'd have done it sooner but I can't move you on my own."

You run thumbs-up.exe and your joints crunch and creak. Your digits stiffen with the function only partially completed. Rhiannon winces.

"Stay still, yeah?"

Rhiannon turns and limps over to where the small human and Todd-dog are, then they lie down next to them. They give you a return thumbs-up.exe before curling up in their long leather coat.

The dilapidated warehouse is open on the south side, shielded from wind by a massive pile of rusting metal, broken auto parts, plastic furniture, and fried electronics. Everything is dust-caked. Inside, a battery-powered lantern illuminates Rhiannon and their brother and dog.

You power off your optics and turn all available energy reserves into core processor functionality. Your body is badly damaged, and you have less than a quarter hour of power cell consumption. It should be enough to look deeper into your memory banks. That activity requires no noise. You rotate your head so your scanners are directed at the warehouse opening in case of threats.

Then you search again in the info Alicia McReedy left you.

There is an entry for "lung," the breathing apparatus installed in humans directly from infant-build. You once had an aerial gas dispenser to disable the lung function, before you broke all your weaponry protocols.

PROTOTYPE:
LUNG REGENERATION THERAPY.

It has tags for cancer research, pneumonia, respiratory disease, and air pollution defense. You quickly scan the entry.

CLASSIFIED MATERIAL.
FOR INTERNAL USE ONLY.

Kendra Thomanson in the R&D sector was pioneering the serum for universal lung repair in the Ngo-Yu Medical Research and Technology Laboratory. The facility is listed as OBSOLETE. There is a note attached to the file's meta data.

Hey Mom, I know I'm not supposed to bypass security protocols like this, but the lab is in lockdown after the first attacks, and this is the only way I can message you. So screw it. Yeah, I'm scared but I'll be okay. Olivia is here; she snuck in just before the quarantine. You taught me to love science, and it's gonna pay off. I've figured out the hiccup that was resulting in pleurisy in some cases.

Talk about timing, right? Bombs going off, the world ending, but hey, I found the cure for lung disease and at least my wife is beside me! Maybe when the chimpanzees evolve and take over, they'll find a use for it, haha. Don't blame me, you're the one who showed me those movies at too young an age. ;)

Me, flippant in the face of disaster? I get it from you. I love you, Mom. Olivia sends her love too. Just want to make sure you know. All my notes are attached in the file "green bean casserole recipe." Please try to stay safe. We'll find somewhere to ride this out. See you on the other side of the apocalypse. <3

If you can find Kendra Thompson, or other human scientists like Alicia McReedy, you can give them this data.

Rhiannon does not need to shut down forever.

You come online again to sounds of respiratory distress.

Rhiannon doubles over, coughing. Todd-dog makes distressed sounds and licks their face. The child-human, Parker, stares up at you. They do not talk.

"I hate this," Rhiannon says, their voice modulated low. "Pa got taken by the dust-lung and I'm all we got left. New Gilgamesh is five hundred fricking miles away. Last broadcast said they weren't be sending out more search parties. Too much of a resource drain. Folks gotta come *there*."

Parker wraps their arms around themself and rocks back and forth on their heels. Todd-dog lays down on their toes, head on Rhiannon's leg.

Hydraulic fluid leaks from Rhiannon's optics. "I told Pa I'd take care of Parker and I… I…" They cough heavily again. "Iron Man could've saved us, but I'm not even close. He could've flown us all the way to safety."

You do not want Rhiannon to shut down. If there is a broadcast by other humans, you should be able to intercept it. You set your unstable tuner to autoscan for messages and survey the warehouse.

The structure was built up over the giant X you were shot on. Makeshift walls of sheet metal and plastic are pasted over I-beams and skeletal rafters. Junk is everywhere; you notice the end of one cannon barrel was repurposed as a support near one corner. You look away.

A radio signal squiggles within your search range, and you copy it immediately to long-term storage.

This is New Gilgamesh. We are a safe harbor for any survivors. If you receive this message, we urge you to come to the following coordinates. A GPS string follows. We have shelter, food, medicine, and clean air. We are a peaceful cooperative of scientists and farmers and believe everyone can contribute to a new world. We welcome everyone. Together, we survive. Come home.

It is four-hundred-sixteen miles southwest.

You ping Rhiannon. <NON-HOSTILE WILL ASSIST. DELIVER HUMANS AND DOG TO SANCTUARY FOR REPAIRS.>

They raise their head, blinking away fluids. "Hey, man, you might be a walking tank, but that ain't doing us no good."

You are not supposed to counter human input, but you were also supposed to destroy things, not save them. You are large enough to carry two humans and a dog.

You begin dragging yourself towards the exterior, where your batteries can fully recharge.

It takes you thirteen hours of careful labor to construct the wagon.

You salvage a bus frame and bend scrap metal into makeshift wheel treads; you find old chain and pipe and weld the harness to your non-functional arm with a repurposed plasma cannon in your wrist. You are not made for finesse.

The wagon is half again as long as you are tall, blocky and full of holes. Once they see what you're doing, Parker assists you by piling the inside with fiber materials for impact reduction.

Parker doesn't use their built-in vocal processor; that is okay, since you don't have one, either. Parker is much more agile and skilled than you, and they understand on an intuitive level how to help.

You find a plastic window mostly intact, and mount it on the front of the wagon to minimize dust kickback into the interior.

Rhiannon stands in the warehouse opening, clutching their tool belt and staring at the vehicle. "You made that?"

You carefully run thumbs-up.exe; you've slowed down your reactions so it doesn't look aggressive. Parker mimics you with both hands. You're very proud of them.

"Wow," Rhiannon says. "Are you… gonna take us to New Gilgamesh?"

You nod once. Parker found some grease and climbed on you while you took short breaks to let the solar cells recharge, and they lubricated your rough joints so you have better articulation.

Parker slaps their leg with one hand, summoning Todd-dog, and together they climb into the wagon. The dog runs excitement-tail.exe, which you determine is positive.

Slowly, Rhiannon limps over and pulls themself into the wagon. You pivot, gathering up the harness, and pull.

The wagon creaks rhythmically behind you as you trudge along the long-abandoned roads.

Two days later, the silhouette of New Gilgamesh looms before you. The sky is overcast, but your batteries are still at fifty-percent. You've moved at a steady pace to conserve energy. The broadcast washes over you and you stop a quarter mile from the gates.

You don't know if there are G-X77 cannons mounted by the entrance. You don't want to be shot again. Rhiannon might not be able to fix you.

"What's the matter, Steadyboi?"

You've sent Kendra Thompson's lung regen files to Rhiannon's tablet, so they have the backup in case you get destroyed. You point at your non-functional arm.

Rhiannon frowns, shielding their eyes as they peer up at you. Parker hugs Todd-dog and waits.

How do you explain being scared? The painted messages on your chassis have eroded during the time you were shut down.

You look like a warbot.

<NON-HOSTILE. DOES NOT WISH FOR DESTRUCTION.>

Rhiannon limps over to you, reaches up, and pats your hand. "No one's gonna scrap you, Steadyboi. I'll protect you." They hold onto your arm. "Like Iron Man would."

Parker nods. Todd-dog barks.

With your humans on either side of you and Todd-dog trotting along beside Parker, you lumber forward, still dragging the wagon.

"Hey!" Rhiannon cups their hands around their mouth to project their voice. "We come seeking sanctuary! Don't shoot our bot. He's friendly."

You broadcast a hesitant message. <HUMAN NEEDS LUNG REPAIR. DATA ATTACHED.>

You send Kendra Thompson's files.

The gates swing open and four adult-model humans rush out; they carry plastic boxes with MEDICAL printed on the sides. You stay motionless. You've gotten Rhiannon and Parker and Todd-dog here. As long as they are safe, well, it won't be so bad if the cost is you getting scrapped again.

An adult-model human in a white lab coat like Alicia McReedy once wore marches out as the medics inspect Rhiannon and Parker. "How did you get my files?"

You don't dare move, with so many humans clustered around you.

The human in the white coat types on a tablet, and the text message pings you.

I'm Kendra. I helped found this place as a sanctuary. Did you know my mom?

You send back: <NON-HOSTILE WAS MADE BY ALICIA MCREEDY.>

Wow. I never thought any of her bots survived.

<CAN HUMAN RHIANNON BE REPAIRED?>

Kendra Thompson nods. They smile at Rhiannon and Parker and Todd-dog. "We've dedicated a lot of resources to the lab. My treatment works for dust-lung. You'll be okay, friends."

To you, Kendra Thompson says, "You rescued these people and brought them here safely. Not an easy feat these days."

You scan the area, nervous that cannons will rise from the walls.

<STEADYBOI HAS NEW PURPOSE. HELP HUMANS.>

"Come on in, Steadyboi," Kendra Thompson says. "I think we could find a job for you. My mom would be proud. You're built tough. How do you feel about helping us find other survivors and bringing them home?"

Parker hops up and down, nodding. Rhiannon has a mask over their nose and mouth, an air canister feeding them oxygen. The medical humans wave everyone towards the gates.

Kendra Thompson watches you, waiting.

You get to choose who you are.

<STEADYBOI WILL HELP.>

And you run thumbs-up.exe.

The Frequency of Compassion

Kaityn Falk loves the dark phase of the moon[1].

It's quiet. Soothing. Insulated in their spacesuit, comm dimmed, Kaityn sits in the rover and watches the sky. Here on Io 7, a newly discovered satellite in retrograde orbit around a dwarf planet the size of Pluto, they are the only living human in several thousand lightyears. They are here to establish research beacons for star-charting, a risky job for how isolated it is—and Kaityn hasn't loved anything this much in their life. The exhilaration of travel, the calmness of

[1] CN: misgendering, threats of violence, non-consensual telepathic contact, mention of parent death

deep space, the possibility of an ever-unfolding universe.

"Daydreaming again?"

The onboard nav AI, Horatio, is the exception to Kaityn's preference for silence. Developed with multi-faceted personality modes to stem off homesickness and loner's fright, the AI is Kaityn's co-pilot, research assistant, and friend.

"Just dreams," they reply. "Wouldn't it be cool if we evolved in a way to survive vacuum and could sail around without spacesuits?"

"Technically, I already can," Horatio says.

Kaityn laughs. "When I was a kid, I wanted to grow giant dragonfly wings in order to zip around in zero-G. I guess hyperdrive is close enough."

The vast scope of sky, its silken blackness, rocks Kaityn in a serene, wordless lullaby. These few hours between the rotation from dark to light on Io 7 are theirs, and they bask in the solitude. There are plenty of other taxing, long-distance meetings and digital paperwork to dull their enthusiasm of being in space, on the rim of the Milky Way. This time is theirs.

In another two weeks, they will begin the trip to Mars HQ to reorient and decompress from a six-month shift. Kaityn sighs. They don't like thinking about the inevitable burst of human interaction they will have to bear for half a year before they can travel again.

"You seem melancholy," Horatio says. The AI's voice is warm against Kaityn's ears inside their helmet. "Is something distressing you?"

"Just thinking about how little time we have left on this shift."

Kaityn is autistic and hyperempathic. When they were young—before they knew they were agender, before they had words for why they always felt so keenly for everyone around them—they coped badly. So much sound, so much light, so many shades of *emotion*. It was the promise of cold, isolated quiet in space that drew them to the Galactic Exploration for Peace agency. GEP needed people willing to risk the vast expanse on the edges of known space.

Out here, Kaityn can *breathe*. They can serve humanity without being overwhelmed by everything that makes humans imperfect and wondrous.

"I'm programmed to list the benefits of six months on, six months off duty," Horatio says, "but I suspect that is unhelpful."

Kaityn smiles wanly. "I'll figure out something—"

A bright wisp flickers across their helmet's viewscreen. It moves too fast for them to define it—but its distress radiates sharp like a needle. Kaityn straightens with a gasp. "Horatio, did you pick that up on scanners?"

"Yes, I did," Horatio says.

"What's your take?"

"It touched down two kilometers from your position. Odd energy reading, extremely small mass. There should be no minor satellites in decay orbit."

"It feels alive." Kaityn ignites the solar engines and guides the rover along the path Horatio provides via map readouts. "And it's hurt."

Their thoughts blur with sudden excitement. *Alive.* Could this be potential first contact?

Protocols rush through their mind. Establish sensory verification if possible: auditory, ocular, olfactory, tactile, light spectrum, mechanical observation, recordable frequencies; identify yourself and designation but do not engage in any negotiation without authorization—

Kaityn's pulse races. They shouldn't assume anything: maintaining objectivity is the leading tenet for space exploration. It's hard when so many ideas are flooding their brain, the adrenaline spike intoxicating.

"Better hurry," Horatio says. "I've just detected ZeroGen Corps' beacons; their vessel has also picked up the signal."

Kaityn's shoulder twitches in surprise, the emotion bleeding fast into sharp fear. "Why are they in this sector? No reports were logged!"

ZeroGen personnel, unlike Kaityn and members of the GEP, always explore with weaponry ready. ZeroGen Corps is a multinational conglomerate for profit-based space exploration. But there are *rules*, regulations, responsibilities. Any human-piloted expedition or spaceflight is supposed to be logged on a public records database. If ZeroGen is out here incognito, they are disregarding all safety protocols. Why?

"They are not responding to my hailing request," Horatio says. "Please proceed with caution."

Kaityn swallows. "I will."

The sense of *pain* grows stronger as Kaityn approaches the signal.

The rover purrs over the rocky surface of the moon. Kaityn remembers playing the old video game series *Mass Effect,* where they piloted an indestructible ground vehicle. They reveled in flying it off cliffs just to watch the absurdity of low-G and unbreakable shock absorbers. They aren't nearly as reckless with an actual GEP-commissioned rover—especially when they're driving, and this is reality. Still, in private, Kaityn thinks of their rover as the Mako 2.0.

Dust kicks up behind the treads, and on the radar map, Kaityn notes the signal lit up as a green flare. They park the rover half a kilometer away and strap on their survival/first aid pack.

The vibrations of *hurt-lost-scared* presses against their consciousness even this far away. They swallow hard, their throat tight.

In space, they have only their own emotions to process. This nervousness is all theirs. Although Kaityn believes AIs have cognition and emotion, Horatio operates on a different frequency from their perception. They asked once if that was intentional to accommodate them. There was a long pause—for Horatio, at least—and then the AI replied: "Yes, I do. I was not programmed to project emotions, merely to observe and respond to them when appropriate."

"But you're *full* of sensors," Kaityn said, flapping their hands in excitement. "And you do feel—I can tell by the way you operate. We might be similar in that way."

"Interesting analysis," Horatio said. "Perhaps we are both outliers from how we were originally programmed."

Kaityn liked that: another thread of connection between them and Horatio.

Now, Kaityn struggles to rein in their wildly fluctuating emotional response. This could be first contact! The sheer thrill is muted with fear, and the building sense of *pain* they can't ignore, like an oncoming migraine.

Kaityn unstraps from the rover and hops out.

Their boots leave quarter-inch tracks in the soft moon dust. Kaityn resists the urge to flop down and roll around, making an angel pattern in the sediment. It isn't polite to the moon, and they can't spare the time.

They're reminded of fresh, soft snowfall in North Dakota, where they lived as a child. They would bundle up in a plush jacket, snow pants, mittens, hat—always refusing a scarf for how it itched against their skin—and dash out into their huge yard. After a snowfall, there was a sense of calm and serenity under the vast gray sky. They would flop in the beautiful drifts, gather clumps of snow to make forts or dinosaurs until called back inside when their lips grew numb and their cheeks turned bright red.

Winters were never the same for Kaityn when they moved to Chicago at age ten, and there was no peace under the sky.

Kaityn navigates via digital map and their helmet's built-in spotlights. Mesas sprout up and meld into cliff faces on Io 7's surface. Their helmet light casts jagged shadows along the gray-blue stone. There: a disturbance in the arid stone. Dust sways like smoke suspended over dimming embers. Something bright and translucent shimmers within a tiny crater, a crack in the stone.

Pain.

It makes Kaityn flinch: the intensity is needle-hot, cascades of glass fragments carried in ice water. *Alone. Lost. Help.*

"I'm coming," Kaityn calls aloud, aware that whatever it is, it may not understand vocal resonance or language constructed for human tongues and minds and hands. Protocol states any approach should be made with caution and only as a last resort if visual, verbal, or mechanical hailing signals do not produce a verifiable response. But they can't wait. They break into a run, the low gravity carrying them in long, effortless leaps across the remaining distance.

"I advise caution," Horatio says. "Even if unintentional, a distressed life-form may prove dangerous."

"I know."

"Overriding internal contact failsafe," Horatio says. "I will abide by your discretion."

Kaityn didn't know the AI could do that, but right now, they are too focused on reaching the life-form and aiding in whatever manner they can.

Kaityn narrows their eyes as they approach, dimming their helmet light to the lowest setting. It takes a second to control their momentum and balance theirself. They hold their hands away from their body, heart pounding, and edge around the last chunk of rock between theirself and the hurt life-form.

It is octagonal light, soft-edged, with undulating ripples along the surface. Perhaps two feet in diameter, with no visible protrusions or indentations. Yet it has mass, for it is partially buried under crumbled rock and dust, and it is hurt.

Kaityn takes slow, deep breaths, centering theirself and trying to control their vocal tone.

"My name is Kaityn Falk," they say as they edge nearer. GEP protocol dances in their foremost thoughts, ingrained training, and yet the wonder almost closes off their voice. First contact with another being, out here on Io 7. This is real. This is *real*. "I'm a human from the planet Earth, and I mean you no har—"

The alien shape undulates, its light frequency strobing, and it lets out a sound that is not auditory so much as felt in the bones, in the soul. Kaityn screams as the pain hits them—

—breaking away from the cluster, caught in solar winds, tossed and tumbled against ice and void, snagged in gravity, pulled through atmosphere. Where are the others? So alone. Afraid. Lost? How will others find? No communication thread, broken from stress. Falling, matter denser and sensation-undocumented-not-good—

The sensory overload sends Kaityn reeling back, and they collapse.

Kaityn is six again, sitting on the porch of their house with their mom, drinking hot cocoa and watching the aurora borealis dapple the sky with spilled gasoline colors.

"I want to fly in space!" Kaityn declares.

Mom laughs. "What would you do in space?"

"Pick up *all* the colors and put them in a basket and bring them back for you. So you can paint with them!"

"Wow, that's pretty cool," Mom says, grinning. "Are there colors up there I can't find in the art department?"

They nod solemnly. "Those are *space colors,* Mom. You can't buy them in the store."

Mom hugs Kaityn with one arm. "Well, baby, that sounds like a good plan. When you bring me space colors, we'll paint a picture together."

Kaityn beams and finishes the melty marshmallows at the bottom of their mug.

Mom never saw them celebrate their twelfth birthday. Car accident. Kaityn stopped drawing; they would never collect space colors, not when their mom couldn't paint anymore.

In the cluster, we all are connected by billions of threads. We flow ever outward, sharing thought and wonder and memory. Languages saturate our understanding, rich and intricate; trillions of ways for connection, for empathy, for life. We are vastness, we are unity, we are individual. And there is a hole in ourselves: we are missing one of us. This is hurt, this is pain, this is sorrow. We cannot move forward, towards the beginnings and the ends of the universe, until we find ourself. To abandon one is to abandon the cluster. It is not who we are. We will find ourself, ourselves, for one is no greater or lesser than all.

Kaityn often chats online with their boyfriend (before he's their ex) about the possibility of first contact. One day, he says, "You know I support you and all, but what if you were the first person aliens met? Wouldn't being agender just confuse them?"

Kaityn grasps for words, their mouth empty, their brain feeling sluggish and disconnected.

He presses on, his face close to the screen. "I mean. Wouldn't it make more sense, if you met an alien, to explain you were a woman? That way when they encounter the rest of humanity, it wouldn't be as jarring."

Kaityn looks at their hands, their whole body flushed with shame. They can't find a coherent way to explain all that is wrong with his assumptions. Would aliens need to be dual gendered, or even have a concept of gender? Would aliens even need pronouns? All Kaityn's snappy semantic and scientific theories and explanations vanish like a hard drive crash.

"I'm just saying," he says. "You've got to think of what's best for humanity. First impressions only come once."

"I know," they mumble. It's in all the training material for GEP, and they've downloaded and studied it over and over with giddy excitement. There is such possibility in the stars.

"Kaityn," he says. At least he consistently uses their correct name. "You know I care about you. I just want to make sure you're doing what's right."

He's been subtly resistant to their gender and pronoun choices, especially when they legally changed their ID before accepting the position in GEP. Kaityn doesn't want to confront him about it. He gets defensive and asks why they're attacking him over such trivial details. It's his disappointment that always stings the worst.

Kaityn can't shake off the doubts that are always there, in the back of their mind, insidious and small and prone to springing up when they are least prepared. What if he's right? Their chances of encountering alien sapient life are billions to one; yet people still win lotteries. It isn't impossible.

"Okay," Kaityn says then, and mumbles an excuse about a migraine—their head throbs, their eyes sting from withheld tears—and logs off.

"He was bad for you," Horatio says later, when they share that painful story when almost drunk. It's their first week on a solo trip and every time they look at the vast mural of space, they hear their ex's voice and his… concerns. "He wanted the his-version of you, not your true self."

"Yep," Kaityn agrees. "Should have dumped his ass long ago." Their voice doesn't have the conviction they want, but it feels good to say aloud nonetheless.

Kaityn blinks against the searing light-pain in their eyes. They're lying just outside the crevice where the life-form crashed; their suit's readings show no physical damage, and the timestamp in their helmet's log indicates barely thirty seconds have passed.

"Kaityn? Kaityn?" Horatio sounds deeply concerned. For a moment, Kaityn feels the AI's worry like an ache in their jaw, spreading down their neck. "Your biorhythms and brainwaves were erratic and completely inconsistent with human physiology. I was afraid you were dying. I have sent distress signals on all frequencies."

Carefully, Kaityn sits up. They want to rub their face, dig their thumbs against the cheekbones and sinuses to alleviate the throbbing pressure. Their helmet prevents them. Gloves too insulated, no skin contact. Their vision normalizes, the afterimages of falling stars and sun flares dissipating into memory. The suit injects a mild painkiller and a faint whiff of lavender into their oxygen supply. It's the scent Kaityn likes most, and they have the dosage perfectly balanced so it won't overwhelm them.

"I'm… okay…" Kaityn blinks again.

We are so sorry, says the light still trapped in stone.

Kaityn's whole body shivers and their shoulders hunch up in excitement.

"Horatio?" Kaityn whispers. "Do you hear that?"

"I do," the AI says. "There is no auditory or digital relay for this communication, however, at least that my sensors can detect. It is… not a phenomenon I am programmed to understand. Is this telepathy?"

In a sense, the voice says.

It is soft, like a pillow wrapped in microfiber and with no aroma.

We did not intend you harm. We bonded thoughts without your consent, and we are deeply ashamed of this. We ask forgiveness for such violation.

Kaityn shakily regains their feet and edges nearer to nu. The knowledge of the cluster's pronouns—the cluster and this individual alike—feels natural. Nu broke free of nur clusterselves and fell. Nu is alone here, unsure where nur otherselves are now. It was not an intentional fall—nu simply wished to reach out to the colors of the universe, the beautiful radiance that shimmers between folds of vacuum.

"Wow," Kaityn breathes. Their thoughts spin in ecstatic patterns, like small shiny cubes all clanking together. They resist flapping their hands, even if it makes their arms ache. "Wow."

Nu is still trapped under the outcropping of moon rock.

They need to focus. Their GEP training is a solid grounding point: in an emergency, remember to breathe. Oxygen for the brain. Appraise the situation. Your kit and vehicles are equipped with a wide range of multi-situational tools. Your AI co-pilot will assist you.

They kneel by the rocks. Their kit has a collapsible pole for a mobility aid. It'll work well as a pry-bar. Kaityn withdraws the metal tube and snaps it open.

"I'm going to loosen the rocks," Kaityn says, their voice shaking. "I'm going to move slow so more debris doesn't fall."

Understanding shimmers from the life-form.

Gingerly, Kaityn digs the tip of the pole into a crevice where the largest rocks are pinning the life-form's body. "Is there anything I can do to ease your pain?"

Not alone, nu says. *Enough for...* It flickers, the pain flaring and dimming. Kaityn gasps and flinches. Tries to steady their hands and push past the hurt.

"Alert: ZeroGen Corps' shuttle is in orbit and locked onto our location," Horatio says.

Kaityn bites the inside of their cheek by accident, and a sharp tingle of pain makes them wince. They scrabble to get leverage on the stone without harming the life-form or causing more rocks to fall.

You show distress, nu says, and sends *concern-for-well-being* and offers *soothing-calm-serenity.* Kaityn hesitates: the emotions hover in soft swirls, like fresh watercolors held in little paper cups. They accept a sip of *soothing-calm,* if only to steady their nerves. Peace settles inside their mind, and their bio-rhythms smooth. Their focus sharpens. There, mapped out like a puzzle's answer, they see where they need to apply leverage to the moon rock and shift it so the low gravity will roll it safely away and let nu free.

"Thank you," they say aloud, and nur light tones warm in mutual pleasure to have helped them. Nu is transferring nur pain inward so as not to distract and cause harm to Kaityn. They smile shakily in gratitude.

With a slow tumble and spray of dust, the rock shifts and the life-form lies bare and exposed. Kaityn pulls out an emergency solar blanket and drapes it across nur body.

Nu sends *thankfulness* to them.

And then ZeroGen Corps arrives.

Dust gusts and spins in angry patterns, violently disturbed as a militarized shuttle drops from orbit and blasts the surface without care or consent of the moon.

Kaityn flings an arm up in reflex.

"Step away from the alien." The ZeroGen operator's signal blasts into Kaityn's frequency. "It is being claimed by ZeroGen Corps for scientific study."

Kaityn winces in pain and freezes. Their suit compensates for the decibel level over the channel and drops it until they can hear and aren't overwhelmed by the noise. They raise their hands, the protocol for a GEP employee's non-hostile acknowledgment and negotiation tumbling in tangled patterns through their head.

There are five operators: all in dark-tinted armor and helmets, armed with electric bolt guns, and radiating *intensity* tinged with *hostility* and *nervousness*. The ZeroGen personnel have already logged the signal and site; if they don't return with evidence, or secure the asset, they'll be docked and fined.

"I'm Kaityn Falk from—"

"We know who you are," snaps the operator who spoke first. "GEP outposts are noted on this moon but you haven't tagged the alien for official observance. Move away from it now."

"Nu," Kaityn corrects, and then realizing the operator may not understand, they add, "Nur pronouns are—"

"Alert!" Horatio beeps in alarm. "Weapons armed!"

The lead operator shoulders their bolt gun and aims at Kaityn's torso. The ZG-X24 model: it has enough force, even in low gravity, to damage or rupture their spacesuit. Worse, Kaityn is alone except for Horatio, who is incorporeal, and if ZeroGen intends to harm them, it's no stretch to assume the operators would also disable the AI and leave no contestable record of illegal activity. Horatio has sent an emergency ping, yes, but signal still takes time to traverse space, and by then it will do Kaityn and Horatio and nu no good.

Kaityn's pulse flutters, a rush of blood in their ears. They can't hold down their terror, the sudden, visceral realization they might die here on this moon, and it will be weeks before the next scout ship reaches them. Days before anyone knows something's wrong when they don't log a report update. Unknown span of time where their body will freeze from depressurization.

Yet worst of all is knowing that if ZeroGen captures nu, nu will be subjected to horrors and pain and *aloneness*.

"I'm sending an additional distress—" Horatio's frequency shorts out. Jamming signal. Kaityn can only hear their own breath, their own thoughts.

Trembling, Kaityn puts one foot before the other. They will not leave nu alone. They will not fight—they're unarmed and outnumbered and have always been a pacifist—but they will not abandon the life-form to cruelty and destruction.

"You are not going to harm nur," Kaityn says. The radio frequency is still open between them and the leader. "Please return to your vehicle and—"

"Step. Away."

Kaityn steps, but they step in front of the light and keep their arms outspread. "No," they say, soft and firm, and press outward with their emotions as steadily as they can. Peace. Calm. Acceptance. They do not want to die afraid; they do not want nu to suffer. "I cannot let you harm nu."

"Fine," the ZeroGen person says.

The leader fires.

We reach across the brightness of space, searching, and we find ourself, ourselves, once again. There! The thread is splintered, an unanticipated fall, suspended in this

chronological moment. We knit closed the hurt and we see ourself huddled beside the otherselves. There is distress and fear in all the selves that are not ourselves, and we see the patterns unwind from one self: violence intended. This self acts from bitterness, willingly, and the self's anger radiates outward like the self's weaponry. We sing sadness for this self, this lost one that is not ourselves, for they are alone and do not understand the harm they bring themself when they aim such violence at others. It is not our preference to intervene, and yet, there is a bright self that stands betwixt the violence and our lost self, and we will not let them perish.

Kaityn is packing for their shuttle flight to GEP Station, which is in orbit around Mars. They have a list:

- favorite video games stored on a flashmem drive; portable screen and controller
- a tablet loaded with their music library
- plenty of ebooks
- their favorite sweatshirt

- a plush squid named Inky
- headphones

There's room for a few more physical objects before they reach their weight limit in their suitcase and carry-on. Kaityn looks at the sketchpad, yellowed with age, and the cup of colored pencils that have gathered dust on that same shelf for years.

For a moment, they almost reach out and drop the art supplies in their bag. Mom isn't here to see this. Mom would have loved every minute of packing, departure, hearing the updates, even waiting on lag from text and compressed video messages from Earth to the station.

Mom would have been so proud.

Kaityn leaves the remainder of their weight limit unfilled. They haven't drawn or colored since they were a child. There's no point in trying again.

The universe is bright.

Warmth and love and protection flare around Kaityn. They gasp. Relief: strongest, with the mellow undertones of *welcome* and *we found you!*

Kaityn blinks rapidly, trying to ground theirself in the sudden flood of emotion and light.

The ZeroGen Corps unit is suspended in a shimmery bubble. The electric bolt drifts away, freed from trajectory, left to float calm and cold in space.

"Their vitals and brain waves are stable," Horatio reports, "and it appears to be a state similar to cryo-stasis."

"You're all right," Kaityn breathes.

"I am. Are you?"

Slowly, Kaityn shifts their gaze upward.

The sky is bright with bodies of light, *the cluster*, for nur family has come to find nu.

Their chest squeezes in excitement, in wonder. A vast cloud of light, all hues and tones and shades—so many distinct selves within a whole—

We greet you, the cluster says. A chorus, a unity of voices in cascading music.

Kaityn's mouth hangs open and they slowly lift a hand towards the cluster. "Hello..."

Then nu floats beside them, free of the moon rock, and Kaityn turns their head to meet nu. Their blanket is folded neatly at their foot.

Thank you for your aid, Kaityn Falk. Nur voice is one and many.

"I... think we're... even," Kaityn manages. "You saved me, too."

Nu, and nur cluster above, stretches out a fan of synapses, tendrils of light that coil and drift in the vacuum before Kaityn's helmet.

We wish to share views from the universe as we have traveled, the cluster says.

Kaityn gasps, nods, and lets the light twirl around their helmet. "Can I see... can I see them later?" They're on the edge of a crash, overwhelmed, and they don't want to collapse under the pressure of so much input and sensation.

Whenever you choose to see, they are yours, the cluster says.

"If I may," Horatio says. "There is still the ZeroGen team to deal with. I have logged a complaint about the hostile interaction we have experienced on Io 7."

Kaityn turns back towards the suspended soldiers.

They intercepted ourself's cries when we separated, nu says. *They followed us when we fell.*

That makes sense to Kaityn. Even if ZeroGen didn't feel nur distress, the energy reading would explain how they arrived so fast, if they were already in the sector—chasing an unknown signal the way Kaityn did.

"What will you do with them?" Kaityn asks the cluster.

We will carry them back to their base of operations and release them from stasis, nu replies. *They will not be harmed, and their memories will not be tampered with. They will simply have wasted fuel and resources in this endeavor to do harm.*

Kaityn lets their breath out in relief. "Thank you. For not hurting them."

There is no value in violence, nu says. Its sum equals only pain, and we do not wish to bring pain upon anyone. We hope, in time, your people will understand this.

"I hope so too."

Nu floats upwards into nur cluster, is welcomed back with affection and joy, and reconnects into the synaptic threads of the whole.

The ZeroGen team is pulled gently into the light, along with their shuttle.

"Will we see each other again?" Kaityn asks.

Naturally. The cluster gives off pleasant, soothing reassurance. We are part of the universe and so are you. We continue onward. So do you.

"I'd like that," Kaityn says, and lifts their hand to wave. It's not goodbye; it is *until we share again.*

"This will be quite the report," Horatio says as Kaityn begins their careful walk back to their rover. They've repacked the emergency blanket and will clean moon dust off it later.

They need to lie down; the overstimulation is fast catching up to them and it will take six hours or more of sleep to compensate for the effects of the encounter. Then they will self-soothe by playing one of their favorite video games installed in their quarters: the newest *PuzzleCroft*, or the Star Harvest sim. They'll need to decompress over the next few days, too, and access Horatio's self-care subroutines to help them process all of this. They nearly died, and that isn't a shock easily brushed aside.

"GEP will be..." Kaityn leans against the hood of the rover. They're still aware of the shimmering halo-effect around their helmet, the gifted glimpses of the universe. For later, when they can savor and appreciate the offering in full.

"Excited?" Horatio offers. "This is confirmed first contact with another sentient extraterrestrial species."

Kaityn is too tired to parse the correct words. This is first contact, yes; their helm cam will display a visual and auditory record, and Horatio—

Horatio. Kaityn's face heats with sudden embarrassment. "I've never asked you if you have pronoun preference, Horatio. I'm so sorry."

"Apology accepted, and please do not berate yourself," the AI says. "While my programmers coded me as male due to, I assume, an overwhelming influence of male-ID'd droids in popular media, I've come to think of myself as ze/zir."

Their heart swells, bolstered by hope, relief, and kinship. Kaityn grins. "That's awesome."

"Indeed," ze says.

"With your corroboration and my helm feeds and report, I think GEP will believe us. Perhaps one day, nu and nur cluster will visit us all."

"That is my wish, too."

"Horatio," Kaityn asks as they steer their rover back towards their ship, "do we have any art supplies aboard?"

"Affirmative," ze replies. "GEP regulations do allow for a percentage of cargo weight to be allotted to creative pursuits vital for mental health. There are markers, paper, and a paint app tablet aboard. Plan to take up drawing?"

"More like resuming," Kaityn says. "I once told my mom that when I fly in space, I'd collect all the colors for her." They can see more shades and hue in the sky, in the dust, in the distant gleam of stars. Another small gift the cluster left them. "It's time to keep that promise."

The dark phase of the moon is turning towards the bright star, and soon it will be dawn.

ACKNOWLEDGMENTS

I want to thank all my friends who've stuck with me and offered support, advice, cheerleading, critique, memes, jokes, and best of all their kindness and friendship. Cheers to my buddies at the pub and discord and everywhere else!

Also, gratitude to the various editors who have published my work, helped shape each story into the best version of itself—editors are magic! Thanks for taking a chance on my words.

And finally, I want to thank my parents, especially my mom, who was my first "Supreme Editor-In-Chief," and whose unwavering support and encouragement helped me flourish into the writer I am today. (See? All those trips to the copy shop did pay off!)

Thanks, Mom. :)

Individual Publication Info

"This Cold Red Dust" first published in *My Battery Is Low And It Is Getting Dark*, ed. by Crystal Sarakas & Joshua Palmatier. © 2020 by Merc Fenn Wolfmoor

"it me, ur smol" first published on mercfennwolfmoor.com. © 2018 by Merc Fenn Wolfmoor

"Behold the Deep Never Seen" first published in AVATAR, INC., ed. by Ann Vandermeer. © 2020 by Merc Fenn Wolfmoor

"Housebot After the Uprising" first published on Patreon. © 2017 by Merc Fenn Wolfmoor

"Bring the Bones That Sing" first published in Diabolical Plots. © 2020 by Merc Fenn Wolfmoor

About the Author

Merc Fenn Wolfmoor is a non-binary, queer fiction writer from Minnesota, where they live with their two cats. Merc is the author of two collections, ***So You Want To Be A Robot*** (2017) and ***Friends For Robots*** (2021), as well the novella ***The Wolf Among the Wild Hunt***. They have had short stories published in such fine venues as *Lightspeed, Nightmare, Apex, Beneath Ceaseless Skies, Escape Pod, Diabolical Plots,* and more.

Visit their website: **mercfennwolfmoor.com** for more, or follow them on Twitter **@Merc_Wolfmoor**.

Also By
Merc Fenn Wolfmoor

COLLECTIONS

So You Want To Be A Robot: 21 Stories

These Imperfect Reflections

[forthcoming 2022]

THE SCYTHEWULF CHRONICLES

The Wolf Among the Wild Hunt

The Wolf Against the Court of Stone

[forthcoming 2022]